THE CASE OF THE PURLOINED PARROT

The Case of the Purloined Parrot

A McGurk Mystery

BY E. W. HILDICK

MACMILLAN PUBLISHING COMPANY
New York

Macmillan Publishing Company
866 Third Avenue, New York, NY 10022
Collier Macmillan Canada, Inc.
Printed in the United States of America

10 9 8 7 6 5 4 3 2

The text of this book is set in 12 point Caledonia.

Library of Congress Cataloging-in-Publication Data
Hildick, E. W. (Edmund Wallace), date.
    The case of the purloined parrot :
a McGurk mystery / by E. W. Hildick.   p.   cm.
    Summary: McGurk and his squad of amateur detectives investigate
an epidemic of disappearing pets in their neighborhood.
    ISBN 0-02-743965-8
    [1. Mystery and detective stories.]   I. Title.
PZ7.H5463Cauh 1990   [Fic]—dc20   89-37924 CIP AC

CONTENTS

THE CASE OF THE
PURLOINED PARROT

1 Officers of the Round Table

"We've been without a case for weeks," said McGurk when he called me up that Saturday morning in early spring.

"So?" I said.

"So here we are, with a whole week's vacation in front of us," he went on. "And the weather is all set to be great."

"Well," I said, "there's nothing much *we* can do about it, is there?"

"No, not *really* . . ." he murmured.

He said it in a way that made me prick up my ears. It was a kind of thoughtful murmur. A murmur that told me, Joey Rockaway, that he had something planned.

And when McGurk has something planned that has nothing to do with a mystery, it usually means one thing.

A special exercise of some kind. Something to sharpen up our detective skills.

"Anyway," he said, "can you come over to my place?"

"I suppose so," I said. "After I've cleaned up my room and done one or two other chores."

"Good!" he said. "Make it as soon as possible."

"But what about the others?" I said. "You've scheduled a full meeting for two o'clock. Won't this keep until then?"

"No," he said. "I want everything to be ready for when the others arrive."

"Everything to be ready?"

"Yes. I'm planning a surprise. I'm planning to give our headquarters a completely new look."

Uh-oh! I thought. Here we go!

Our HQ is the McGurk basement. We have our meetings there. We keep our records there. And we've handled so many cases that there's quite a lot of stuff lying around. Mrs. McGurk had obviously told McGurk to get it cleaned up—or else.

"Lookit, McGurk!" I said. "I know what you're trying to do!"

"*What* am I trying to do, Officer Rockaway?" he asked, very sternly.

"You're trying to get me to help with *your* chores. Well, I've got chores enough of my own, without—"

"What chores?" His voice was raised to a yelp. "Who said anything about chores? Huh? Go on— *what* chores?"

"Like cleaning up your basement and—"

"Forget it!" he said. "I already did it. I had to, otherwise I couldn't have found room for the new— uh—the new—"

"The new what?"

"The new piece of—uh—equipment."

"Oh?" My mind began to run through the possibilities. "A new filing cabinet? A bigger copying machine? A—don't tell me you've managed to get hold of a new *word processor*."

"You'll be able to see for yourself when you get here," he said. "The sooner the better."

I was there at a quarter of eleven, knocking on the basement door and admiring my newly typed notice, stuck on the inside of the glass panel:

HEADQUARTERS
KEEP OUT
THE McGURK ORGANIZATION

PRIVATE INVESTIGATIONS
MYSTERIES SOLVED
PERSONS PROTECTED
MISSING PERSONS FOUND
MONSTERS EXORCISED
SPIES UNMASKED

That was as far down the long list as I was able to read before the door opened and McGurk stood there, grinning.

"You're early," he said, not moving to let me in.

"Yeah, well—"

I was trying to peer over his shoulder. As far as I could tell there was no big item of new equipment there. No green glow from a word processor screen. No gleam of metal from a full-size filing cabinet.

"Well, now that I'm here," I said, "don't just stand there, McGurk. I thought you said—"

"Sorry!" He moved aside. "There! I bet you never thought it would be *this*, did you?"

When I'd stepped inside I saw at once what he was referring to. Instead of the long, narrow table we usually sit around, there was now a battered-looking round table. All the shine had been worn away. The surface was marked with old rings where damp cups and glasses had been put down carelessly. There were cigarette burns at the edges and splashes of dried white paint all across it.

McGurk had already placed the chairs around it, his rocking chair and our five straight-backed ones. There was a slip of paper on the table.

"Is *this* the new piece of equipment?" I said. "What's the big deal about this?"

Still grinning, he passed me the sheet of paper. It was a seating plan.

"It's like King Arthur and his Knights of the Round Table," he said.

I said nothing as I studied that plan. Here is a copy:

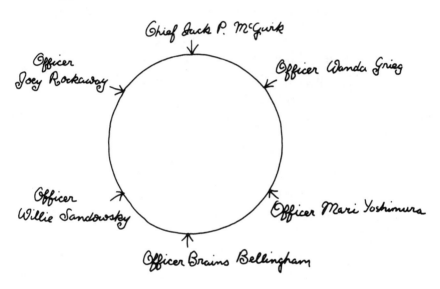

"There, you see," he said. "Everybody equal. No one at the head of the table, no one at the bottom."

I glanced at the chairs.

"I see you've got the rocking chair in *your* place, McGurk."

His grin wobbled some. "Well—yeah. I always

use that. Like—like probably King Arthur had his throne drawn up to the table. It's the rest of you that are equal."

"Hmm!" I said. Somehow I couldn't see the others letting *that* pass.

He must have been reading my thoughts.

"Anyway, to stop any argument, I thought we'd make some place markers and—"

"I doubt whether that would—" I began.

"Hear me out," he said, with a bright green gleam in his eyes. "I'm talking place markers *interesting* enough to keep them busy."

"Like what, McGurk?"

"Like pictures of shields. Like what Ms. Brown was telling us about in class. How knights used to have pictures on their shields showing their life stories."

"Life stories?" I said. "She was talking about family backgrounds. Coats of arms."

"Yeah, well. Whatever. I thought if you could draw one for each of us they'd—"

"Good idea, McGurk!" I said.

I'd already been thinking of what I'd have on my shield. I went into the corner where my typewriter paper was stashed and got six sheets of it.

"Like this," I said, sitting down and beginning to draw.

This is how it turned out:

McGurk's smile broadened again.

"Hey! That's great!" he said.

"Well," I said modestly, dotting in a few lines of writing on the open book, "it certainly describes my job here."

He nodded. Then, frowning slightly, he said, "How about putting a pair of glasses somewhere, with dark rims like yours, to make sure?"

"Knights," I said, "did not wear glasses in those days."

"No, well—what are you writing now?"

I showed him what I had written, just under the shield: *Sir Joey Rockaway, Knight of the Questing Quill and Keeper of the Records.*

"That should make it clear," I said.

He was almost quivering with eagerness now.

"How about doing one for me next?" he said.

"Sure," I said.

I'd had an idea for his, too. For the next few minutes I was busy.

"Well?" I said when I'd finished.

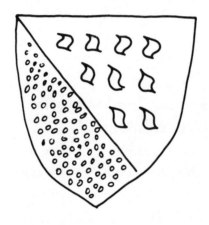

His smile was uncertain.

"What's *that* supposed to mean?" he asked. "Those specks on the left. A swarm of bees?"

"Freckles," I said. "Like yours."

"Huh! And those wavy lines on the right?"

"Flames," I said. "Like your red hair."

Then I wrote under the shield: *Sir Jack McGurk, Knight of the Fiery Freckles.*

"*Sounds* all right," he murmured. "But—"

"But also the freckles *could* be a swarm of bees," I said. "Representing all the dozens of good ideas you come up with."

He was smiling again.

"And the flames are not only your hair," I said. "They're also the way your ideas light things up for the rest of us."

His smile was at its broadest now.

"Well, let's hope *this* idea lights things up this afternoon. You'd better get busy with the other shields."

I already was. All lit up myself . . .

By the time the others arrived, the shields were all done and in the right places.

Wanda Grieg started in criticizing immediately.

"I notice you're still sticking to the rocking chair, McGurk. So which is—oh!"

McGurk and I had decided to fold the names under the shields and see if each person could recognize his or her own emblem. Wanda, the tree lover, had found hers right away. She was already unfolding the name: *Lady Wanda, Warden of the Woodlands.*

"I like it!" she said through the veil of long yellow hair that hung down on the side of her face as she bent over the shield.

"Hey!" someone said, behind me. "He-e-ey!" he said again, in an injured tone.

Willie had found his.

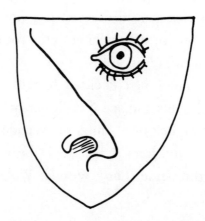

"I know I have a long nose," he said, "but there's no need to make fun of it!"

"Nobody is making fun of it, Officer Sandowsky," said McGurk.

"It just tells what a very sensitive nose you have, Willie," I said. "How you can detect the most delicate smells and recognize them."

"Yeah," said McGurk. "Open up the name part and you'll see."

Willie did this and brightened up at once when he saw the writing: *Sir Willie Sandowsky, Knight of the Seeing Nose.*

Brains Bellingham, our science expert, was the next to protest.

He recognized the science emblems, all right, and approved.

"This flash of lightning stands for my electronic skills, right?" he said. "And this clock thing is meant to be a dial on one of my instruments. I'm not sure about this other—"

"That's a condenser," I said. "Like they have in chemistry labs."

"Condenser!" he jeered. "That's called a *retort*, Joey. I thought you were the word expert! I—"

He broke off. His eyes popped behind his round-lensed glasses. He had flushed to the roots of his short, fair, bristly hair.

He'd opened up the name part.

Master Brains Bellingham, Artificer of Cunning Devices.

It was the "Master" bit that had bugged him. He's a year younger than the rest of us.

"Why can't *I* be a knight, too?" he asked me.

"That's what I asked him," said McGurk. "But it's all right, Officer Bellingham. *Master* is what they called the king's most powerful advisers."

"And his top craftsmen," I added.

"Yeah, well—" Then Brains perked up. "I see now. Yeah."

I think the "Artificer of Cunning Devices" clinched it for him.

So now there was only one shield left. The shield of Mari Yoshimura. The Japanese girl knew at once that the remaining shield had to be hers—but she looked puzzled.

"Mouths?" she said. "And clouds?"

"Those aren't clouds, Mari," I said.

"You could have fooled me," said Wanda.

"Are they supposed to be small retorts?" asked Brains. "To show Mari's link with science. I mean with her father owning all those electronics factories?"

"Clouds! Retorts!" said McGurk. "They're *speech balloons*! My idea. Open up the name part, Officer Yoshimura, and you'll see."

She did this and saw: *Lady Mari, Maid of Many Voices*.

Mari's face now split open in a big smile.

"Ah, yes!" she said.

"But why aren't the speech balloons joined to the mouths?" said Willie.

"Because," I said, "Mari is skillful in *throwing* her voice, not just in imitating other people's voices."

"Anyway, men," said McGurk, "let's take our places and see if we can come up with some ideas for how to spend the next week."

But we'd no sooner sat down than there was a hammering at the door.

"See who it is, Officer Bellingham," said McGurk.

When Brains opened the door he was nearly knocked over, the newcomer came in with such a rush.

It was Ray Williams, his face all twisted with anxiety.

"Hi, Ray!" said McGurk. "What can we—?"

"I've got a case for you, McGurk," said Ray, in his distress clasping his hands together and making his knuckles crack. "A very important, very urgent case!"

2 Cat Rustlers

Ray is only about a year older than most of us, but his thin, hungry-looking face seemed more than ten years older that afternoon. He looked as if he hadn't eaten in days. He probably hadn't slept much, either; there were dark circles under his eyes.

"Sit down," said McGurk. "Draw up that spare stool and tell us about this case you say you have."

Ray's dark eyes flashed. "It isn't what I *say* I have, McGurk. It's what I *do* have."

He looked too distraught to sit down anywhere as he prowled around behind us, this way and that way, cracking his knuckles. I could see then that this might be the main drawback to that table. It seemed like it might affect all distressed clients the

15

same way, causing them to prowl around and around like that and make us dizzy.

"Anyway," said McGurk, nearly going cross-eyed keeping track of Ray, "stand still a minute and tell us what's the trouble."

Ray did stand still for a few moments.

"It's Whiskers. My cat. You know him."

Then Ray went back to his prowling and knuckle cracking.

And we certainly did know Whiskers. Four of us did, anyway, because what we called the Case of the Condemned Cat occurred before Brains and Mari became members of the Organization.

I stepped over to the cardboard boxes where the records are kept. I pulled Whiskers' mug shot and handed it to Brains and Mari.

"That's the animal," I said.

Here is a copy of the document. It was McGurk's idea to make it look like a post office wanted ad.

Whiskers had been accused of killing a couple of white doves, and the McGurk Organization had helped to clear his name.

Ray looked over Mari's shoulder.

"Yeah," he said in a breaking voice. "That's him. Good likeness, too. I took the photographs myself."

His eyes began to fill with tears.

Then he went on prowling.

WANTED FOR MURDER ʌ *(which he didn't do!)*

Cat: male, tabby. Black tiger stripes on
gray-brown background.

Name: Whiskers.

Owner: R. Williams.

Age: Not known -- came to R.W. as fully
grown stray.

"So what has he been accused of killing this time?" asked McGurk.

"Nothing," said Ray. "He's missing. More than two days."

Murmurs of sympathy rose around the table. From *some* of us, anyway. But not McGurk. He said nothing, looking very stern.

"Maybe Whiskers has just gone off temporarily," said Wanda. "You know—paying visits."

Ray stopped.

"Huh? Visits?"

Wanda shrugged. "Yes," she said. "With girl cats."

Ray shook his head vigorously and resumed his prowling.

"No," he said. "Not Whiskers. He's been fixed."

"Could be," I said, "that he's just gone snooping around someone's garage and gotten himself locked in. Maybe the owners went away for a few days."

Ray stopped again and stared at me hopefully.

"Yeah," he said. "That's just what I've been thinking."

"So," said McGurk, "have you asked around?"

Ray turned to him. "Sure I've asked around. But do you know how many garages and sheds and things there are in this town? That's what I've come to you guys for. To hire you."

"*Hire* us?" said McGurk.

"Sure," said Ray. He looked a bit needled. "You make out like you're detectives and—"

"We *are* detectives," said McGurk.

"So I want you to do some detecting," said Ray. "Help me find Whiskers. I mean it says it on your door, doesn't it? Missing Persons Found."

"But Whiskers is a cat, not—" McGurk began.

"He's a person to *me!*" said Ray.

"And me," said Wanda. "And a most lovable, good-tempered person, too!"

"There you go," said Ray.

McGurk gave Wanda a swift, angry glance, then turned back to Ray.

"Anyway, I'm sorry," he said. "We don't do that kind of work anymore. Penny-ante stuff."

Ray stopped and stared at McGurk with a shocked expression and a half-open mouth.

"McGurk!" said Wanda. "We don't have a case right now. Why don't we take this one?"

"Yeah," said Willie, "just to keep us from getting rusty. Maybe I'll be able to sniff him out. You got something with his scent on, Ray?"

"Sure," said Ray, beginning to look more hopeful. "You can shove your nose into his bedding all you want."

"Yes," said Mari. "And I could do my cat noises."

McGurk looked as if he'd just been about to give Willie a piece of his mind. But now he stared at Mari.

"Huh?"

"Yes," said Mari. "Noises like cats. Like this . . ."

And, hardly moving her lips, she gave out with a whole battery of cat noises: cats complaining, cats singing, cats fighting, cats quietly conversing.

Ray smiled. Briefly, but very definitely smiled. "Hey! That's good! Some of those sound just like old Whiskers himself!"

"Thank you," said Mari. "We could go around outside garages and sheds without troubling people, and I could make the noises and see if there's any reply."

Even McGurk was looking more interested. But he shook his head when Ray said, "Great! How about it, McGurk?"

"Sorry," McGurk repeated. "We just don't take that kind of job anymore. It . . . it would be bad for our image."

Ray gave a growl very similar to one of Mari's fighting-cat noises. Kind of liquid but choked up.

"Penny-ante, huh?" he growled at last. "Okay." He suddenly plunged a hand into his back pocket and brought out a scrap of newspaper. "Read *that*!" he said, slapping it down on the table. "From last night's *Gazette*. Maybe it'll help change your mind."

McGurk stared at the clipping, then bent forward, his eyes in green slits as he read it.

Here's a copy:

CAT RUSTLERS BUSY IN JOHNSONVILLE

Our Turn Next?

For the past month, the police in Johnsonville have been trying to track down what is believed to be a gang of cat thieves. Over 30 cases have been logged in the past four weeks.

Vivisectionists?

Says Chief of Police Edgar P. Brown, "We believe they have been stolen for shipping alive to laboratories in New York, where they are used for surgical experiments. It's illegal, of course, but that's what makes it profitable to petty thieves, who can get as much as thirty dollars for each live cat."

Next Stop?

Fortunately for the cat owners of Johnsonville, the spate of thefts seems to be decreasing. But, as Chief Brown pointed out, "This probably means they'll be moving on to another town in the area."

"Read it aloud to us, McGurk," said Brains.

McGurk grunted, then cleared his throat and did as Brains had asked.

"Well?" said Ray, glaring at McGurk when he'd finished reading. "*That's* not penny-ante, McGurk. And"—his voice faltered—"and that's what I'm afraid might have happened to Whiskers. That the rustlers *have* moved on. To *our* town."

McGurk sat back and returned Ray's glare.

"Why didn't you say so before?" he said. "*Sure* we'll take the case! What's more, we'll get right onto it! Okay, men?"

3 Dragnet

Ray didn't stay long after that. He was still very anxious.

"I have to go back just in case someone calls to say they've found Whiskers," he said. "I wrote our phone number on his flea collar."

McGurk was pleased to let him go. He likes to run our investigations his own way, without the clients fussing around. He loves to get out the street map and plan a search stage by stage. Like a dragnet, as he calls it.

That's at the beginning. Later, if there are no signs of success, he drops this approach and works on hunches.

Anyway, that's how the search for Whiskers began. Very methodically.

"You can bet Ray will have covered the streets near his house pretty thoroughly," McGurk said, spreading the map on the table. "But of course he won't have made a real professional job of it. So we'll start by going over the same territory and working our way in toward his house."

Here is a copy of the map for the area he had in mind:

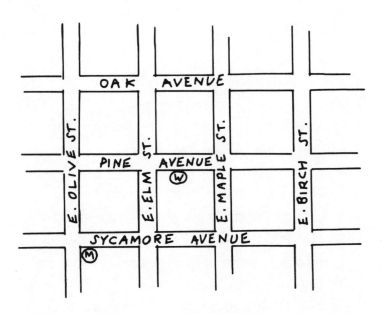

(M) = McGurk house

(W) = Williams house

"Starting here, we work clockwise," said McGurk. "Along East Olive as far as Oak. Then along Oak as far as East Birch, down East Birch as far as Sycamore, and back to here."

"And what are we doing all this time?" asked Wanda.

"Keeping our eyes skinned for garages and sheds that are shut up," said McGurk. "Getting Officer Yoshimura to make her cat noises. Then listening for any reply."

"But won't Ray have been doing that already?" I asked. "Not making cat noises, but calling Whiskers' name?"

"Sure," said McGurk. "But Whiskers might have been sulking or playing games, and keeping quiet on purpose. But when he hears strange *cat* noises— then his curiosity'll get the better of him and he *will* reply."

"What about Willie's nose?" said Brains.

"Yeah!" said Willie, stroking it.

"That's really for later," said McGurk. "For if we suspect a cat might have been shut in someplace, but transferred in the meantime."

"Oh?" said Wanda. "Are you thinking about—"

"The cat rustlers, yes," said McGurk. "You never know. But first we have to check out the accidental-lock-in theory. . . . Anyway, after we've made the first circuit, we continue to search *inside* that area."

We watched as he traced with a freckled finger the route from Sycamore along East Elm as far as Oak . . . then down from Oak to Sycamore along East Maple . . . then finally along Pine from East Birch to East Olive, taking in the Williams house itself.

"At that point we can check with Ray and see if he *has* had a call," said McGurk.

"Stopping by so I can get a good sniff at Whiskers' bedding," said Willie.

"Right," said McGurk. "That's if we haven't already found Whiskers in our dragnet," he added, ever optimistic.

A very neat plan, right?

Nice and clear cut, right?

On paper—yes.

But things don't always work out so tidily when plans like that are put into action.

I mean how could we have known that Mari's cat noises would turn out to be so attractive to cats in general? That she'd attract cats the way the ice-cream truck chimes attract kids? Whenever we saw a closed garage she went into her act, throwing her voice up the driveway, after which we'd listen carefully.

And the response?

Well, let me tell you.

I used the shield device as a kind of shorthand to record this stage of the investigation, and here it is:

For every squawk or meow or yowl or spitting, fighting growl we usually got at least one response— but not from under any closed garage door. Oh, no! From doorsteps, windowsills, the hoods of parked cars—wherever a cat happened to be. Tabbies like Whiskers but with different colors or stripes. Black cats, red cats, calico cats. Old battered tomcats with chewed-up ears and playful kittens. And whenever one of them stepped forward, a cat owner usually wasn't far behind.

And boy, did we get some dirty, suspicious looks!

Like Ray, most of these people had read about the likelihood of cat rustlers coming into the neighborhood, and McGurk had a lot of fast talking to do to convince some of them we were only looking for Ray's cat.

The most startling response, though, didn't come from a cat or a cat owner. It came from the back porch of the house next to Ray's—Mrs. Berg's.

Mari had just thrown an especially plaintive cat call at the bottom of the closed garage door, when the air was split with the most startling screeching sound I have ever heard.

"*Scree-yok-cha-cha-cha-skereech!*"

We froze.

"W-what was *that?*" said Willie.

"It wasn't a cat, that's for sure!" said Wanda.

"It wasn't—uh—human, either!" said Brains, gulping.

"Mari," I said, "it wasn't *you*, was it?"

"No, Joey," she said. She looked as mystified as the rest of us.

"Make another cat noise, Officer Yoshimura," said McGurk.

She did, aiming it at the garage door again.

And again the crazy high-pitched screeching came from somewhere beyond the garage.

"*Scree-scree-yok-chachachachacha.* . . . *How dare you talk to me like that!*"

"*That* was human," I whispered.

"S—sort of," said Willie.

"More like *sub*human," said Brains.

"Come on, let's find out!" said McGurk.

And that's when Ziggy first entered the case.

4 Ziggy

Mrs. Berg is always friendly toward the McGurk Organization. We'd once helped to catch a thief who'd burgled her home. So McGurk wasn't being too pushy in leading the way to the back of the house. In fact, as he said later, he considered it our *duty* to see what crazy person was abusing her in her own backyard.

"*Scree-scree-eech! I gotta get out of here!*" that person was saying—this time in a broken, suffering voice—as we rounded the corner and—

"A *parrot!*" said Wanda.

She was right. The bird was in a cage on top of the porch table. It was a large cage, but the parrot was big, too. As it fluttered its light blue-gray wings and spread its red tail feathers, it seemed to fill that cage.

Mrs. Berg is a pleasant lady with a plump, smooth face. She was sitting on a chair next to the cage, knitting.

"Oh, hello!" she said. "It's you."

The parrot had gotten quiet. It had folded its wings and was back on its perch, with one beady eye fixed on McGurk.

"Yes, ma'am," said McGurk. "We heard this strange voice and—"

"That was Ziggy," said Mrs. Berg. "It's his first time out in the fresh air since I got him. He heard some cat a few minutes ago. He hates cats."

"That's a nice name," said Wanda. "Ziggy."

"Yes, well," said Mrs. Berg, "as a matter of fact it's short for a much longer word."

"Really?" I said.

"Yes," she said. "Uh—let me see if I can remember. Uh—yes—zygodactyl."

"*Ziggy!*" squawked Ziggy.

"It means any bird having two claws at the front of its foot and two at the back," Mrs. Berg continued. "It gives them a better grip for perching."

We looked. Sure enough, Ziggy's feet were the way she'd described them. He lifted one from the perch as we peered at him, as if he was showing off how steady he could hold himself with just one zygodactylous foot.

Then he put the second foot back and slowly but smoothly swung himself upside down, still keeping a suspicious eye on McGurk.

"Does he talk much?" asked Mari.

"You mean *human* talk, honey?" said Mrs. Berg. She shook her head. "Not a whole lot. But he's still quite young. Only three or four years old."

"That bit about how he's got to get out of here—" McGurk began.

"*I gotta get out of here!*" said Ziggy, still upside down.

McGurk smiled uncertainly. "Uh—where did he get that from?"

"Oh, *that!*" Mrs. Berg laughed. "That's from his favorite radio program. One of those where people phone in with their opinions. The host of the show is always saying that, when it gets near the end. Just as he shouts at some of them and asks them how dare they talk to him like that. Ziggy insists I have it on every day."

Brains pointed to the bird. "His claws are black. Is that—ouch!"

Ziggy had suddenly swung upright and pecked at Brains's pointed finger. Brains snatched it away quickly. Willie backed away with equal speed, his hand automatically covering his nose, which had been nearly as close as Brains's finger.

"Oh, dear! You shouldn't have put your finger between the bars!" said Mrs. Berg. "Has he broken the skin?"

"No," said Brains, inspecting the red mark. "But he's sure got one strong beak!"

"Yes, well," said Mrs. Berg, "all parrots have. They use their beaks to help when climbing trees, you know. They dig them into the bark."

"What kind is he, Mrs. Berg?" asked Wanda, looking with new interest at this tree climber.

"An African Gray," said Mrs. Berg. "They're the best talkers. But very expensive. My children got together to buy it for me. They said it would keep me from feeling too lonely."

"How dare *you talk to me like that!"* Ziggy suddenly yelled, one eye on a very startled Willie.

Mrs. Berg smiled.

"And they were right," she said. "Who could feel lonely with *him* around?"

Mrs. Berg has six grown-up sons and daughters. I wondered how much they'd had to pay for the bird. I guessed it must have been quite a big amount if it took six of them to get the money together.

McGurk was looking thoughtful.

"So Ziggy doesn't like cats, huh?" he asked softly, but with a hard gleam in his eyes.

"No," said Mrs. Berg. "He had a nasty experience

with one in his first home. It caught him while he was flying loose."

McGurk nodded, the gleam softening. Mrs. Berg had answered his question without the slightest trace of guilt. Then he gave a start when a quiet calm voice behind him said, "And what is on *your* mind *this* afternoon?"

Mrs. Berg laughed.

"That's the same person he's copying. That's what the man says at the beginning of his show."

It seemed to have recalled McGurk to his main task.

"Well, it's been nice talking to you, Mrs. Berg," he said. "But we have to press on."

To shrieks of *"How* dare *you talk to me like that!"* we made our way back to the street. Ray Williams was waiting for us at the end of the driveway. He was holding an old crumpled sweater.

"I heard your voices from our backyard," he said. "Talking to *her*. I didn't want to butt in. Besides, I wouldn't put it past her to have picked Whiskers up and dumped him miles away. That dumb bird of hers hates cats and—"

"Oh, but Mrs. Berg wouldn't have done a thing like that!" said Wanda.

"Very unlikely," said McGurk. "It did cross my mind, too. But when we were trying to find out who'd framed Whiskers for the dove killing, someone said she was allergic to cats."

"Yes," said Ray. "And that's all the more reason she might have done what I just said."

McGurk shook his head. "She was innocent then and in my book she's innocent now. Someone who's allergic to cats doesn't drive for miles shut up with one."

"Well, maybe not," said Ray. Then he glanced down at the old sweater and looked at Willie. "Anyway, here's some of Whiskers' bedding. You want to take a sniff?"

"I already did," said Willie. "From where I'm standing now. Even when I was at the other end of the driveway—"

"Pow! Yeah!" said McGurk.

It didn't take a sensitive nose, a *seeing* nose, to detect that smell. It *was* very strong, very pungent.

"Spike lavender, right?" said Willie. "What some folks use for keeping bugs away?"

"Yeah, that's right," said Ray. "Tina, my kid sister, thought she'd be doing Whiskers a favor by spraying his bedding with it. Whiskers hated it, wouldn't sleep on it, wouldn't go near it."

"Maybe that's why he's disappeared," said McGurk. "Waiting for it to wear off."

Ray brightened a little.

"I sure hope that's *all* it is!" he said. Then he went back to looking gloomy. He didn't mention the cat rustlers, but they were obviously still on his mind.

"Okay, men," said McGurk. "Let's get on with the search."

We spent the rest of the afternoon patrolling the borders of the neighborhood beyond the area shown on my map. We did this systematically, too, block by block, moving farther and farther away from Ray's house.

"If Whiskers is straying around, lost, it stands to reason he won't be close to home," McGurk said. "So the farther away we get, the better our chances," he added, with his own special brand of optimism that doesn't always seem to make sense, somehow.

"If that's all he *is* doing," said Wanda. "Just straying."

"It's an angle we just have to keep plugging away at," said McGurk. "Until we get a better lead." There was a dogged, determined look on his face. "And tomorrow morning we pick up from where we leave off."

5 Whiskers?

On Sunday morning, McGurk was in such a confident mood that he had Wanda bring the airline tote bag we'd used for carrying Whiskers in that other time.

"Somehow I have a gut feeling that we'll find him today," he said.

And at first it did look promising. The weather was nice and sunny again, and, since it was Sunday, a lot more garages were wide open, with owners washing their cars or doing minor repairs. Also, since it was the first warm spell, other garages had been opened so that the owners could take out garden furniture or wheel out the lawnmowers.

So, with fewer closed garages and sheds to check out, we were able to make much quicker progress.

By half-past ten we'd covered an extra one-block-wide strip on all four sides of the area we'd searched on Saturday.

But McGurk began having doubts.

"Maybe we're not being thorough *enough*," he said.

"I don't see how we could be much *more* thorough," said Wanda.

"Me, either," I said.

"Lend me your notebook and pen, Officer Rockaway," said McGurk. "And I'll show you what I mean."

It made me wince to see such sloppy work being done in my notebook, but he seemed to make good sense. Here is my own copy of what he'd written and drawn:

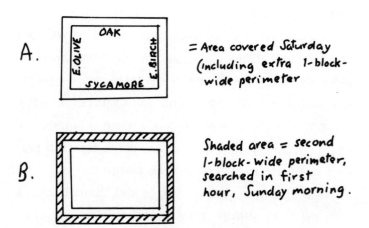

A. = Area covered Saturday (including extra 1-block-wide perimeter

B. Shaded area = second 1-block-wide perimeter, searched in first hour, Sunday morning.

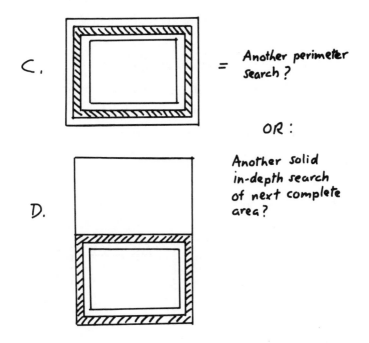

C. = Another perimeter search?

OR:

Another solid in-depth search of next complete area?

D.

"Well, I guess we could waste a lot of time doing the C method," said Wanda. "I prefer D."

"Somehow C doesn't seem to be concentrated enough," said Brains. "With only a one-in-four chance of even being in the right *direction*. I prefer D, too."

"But suppose Whiskers is somewhere below Sycamore instead of above Oak," I said. "Plan D would be a complete waste of time."

"I guess Joey's right," said Willie.

"Yeah," McGurk murmured. "But it's going to

take up a lot of time, going around the edges in thin strips."

It was Brains who finally clinched it.

"Well, if you want my *scientific* opinion, why don't we follow plan D? Except instead of searching the area above Oak, we make it the same size area on the other side of Olive. Like this . . ."

He was even messier in his scribbling than McGurk. Here is my tidied-up version:

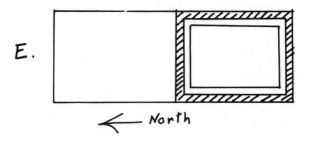

"What makes that any better than plan D?" said McGurk.

"Because it's north of here," said Brains. "Like I've plainly indicated."

"So what makes the area to the north more likely than the one to the east?" said Wanda. "Or west or south, for that matter?"

"Well," said Brains, "I'm only going on what Ray said. About Whiskers being miffed about the lavender spray—you know, sulking."

McGurk's eyes were almost crossing as he looked from Brains to his diagram and back again. "Are you feeling all right, Officer Bellingham?"

"Sure!" said Brains. "If I was a cat and I wanted to get lost, but only *temporarily,* I'd head north."

McGurk frowned. "Why? Why north, Officer Bellingham?"

"Because," said Brains, "the sun would be behind me. So that when I decided to come back I'd know to go *facing* the sun. I mean, sure, it might be too far to the east or west, but at least I'd be in the right *general* direction."

"That sounds very sensible," said Mari. "Very scientific."

"It's better than flipping a coin, I suppose," I said.

"We'll do it, men!" said McGurk. "Even while Officer Bellingham was explaining his scientific theory, I got that gut feeling again!"

Well, scientific approach or gut feeling, neither seemed to be working out as we toiled away, searching area E, that morning and part of the afternoon. But then, when we'd almost covered that area, two incidents raised our hopes.

"Hey!" said Wanda, in a low, urgent voice, as we were walking along a section of Pine Avenue. "Slow down! Do you see what I see?"

The cat was about twenty yards ahead. He'd been ambling along toward us, tail up, just after Mari had produced one of her fruitiest cat warbles. He was a full-grown tabby, with black stripes on a golden-gray background.

And he was wearing a white flea collar.

We all stopped.

And when we stopped, the cat stopped, half crouching, looking at us just as curiously, but cautiously, as we were looking at him.

"What do you think?" I whispered.

"It's Whiskers, all right!" McGurk whispered back.

"Whiskers!" Wanda called softly, holding out her hand. "Here, kitty, kitty! Here, Whiskers!"

The cat blinked at her but otherwise didn't move.

"Men," said McGurk, still in a low voice, "very slowly, very carefully, fan out. Either side of Officer Grieg."

6 Mistaken Identity?

The cat stared at us as, very slowly, very carefully, we fanned out. . . .

Perhaps we went *too* slowly. Perhaps we gave that cat too much time to work out his next move. Because, before that sinister V formation could close in on him, he suddenly took off and sprang up the trunk of one of the trees on that side of the avenue.

"Officer Grieg—" McGurk began.

But our tree-climbing expert had already flung down the tote bag and was shinning up there only a few feet behind the cat.

The cat must have been startled by this. At any rate, he made the mistake of going out on the first limb he came to.

"You've got him now, Officer Grieg!" said McGurk as Wanda reached that limb herself.

We looked up. McGurk seemed to be right. There was nowhere for the cat to go except farther along that limb. The young leaves were only just beginning to break out, so we could see everything very clearly. And, as the cat moved a few feet farther away, he seemed to realize he was trapped. He turned and glared at Wanda, who was now sitting straddling the limb at its thickest part.

"Well, don't just sit there, Officer Grieg," said McGurk. "Go get him!"

"Oh, yeah?" said Wanda. "The limb's bending even with the *cat's* weight."

"So just stay put and wait until he decides to come back," said McGurk.

The cat seemed to understand McGurk's words. As if in answer, he slowly sat down in the network of twigs, still facing Wanda. Then he squeezed his eyes half shut, as if to say: "I don't know about you, miss, but I'm quite comfortable just sitting here. So how d'you like *them* apples?"

"I could be here for *hours!*" said Wanda.

"Why don't you try shaking the branch?" said Brains.

"Why don't *you* try boiling your head?" retorted Wanda.

I guessed she was just beginning to realize how futile it had been to follow the cat up there in the first place.

"Here!" said McGurk, reaching up with the tote bag. "You'd better have this ready for when he does decide to give himself up."

Wanda tossed her hair.

"Are you kidding, McGurk? It's bad enough trying to get a cat into a bag when you're on the ground."

"Well, just grab him and carry him down then," said McGurk.

Wanda didn't even bother to reply.

"She'd get scratched to ribbons, McGurk," I said.

As if Wanda herself had said it, McGurk looked up at her and snapped, "So why go up there at all?"

This time it was Brains who answered for her.

"Just a reflex action on her part, I guess."

"Who's asking *you*?" McGurk said.

"I came up here," said Wanda, slowly and deliberately, "so I could get a closer look at him." She leaned forward. "To make sure it *is* Whiskers."

"Can you smell lavender?" asked McGurk.

"No," she said. She checked the forward movement of her head. The crouching cat's shoulders had started to take on that spiky, bristly look. His eyes were wide open again. "Can *you*?"

McGurk turned. "Officer Sandowsky?"

Willie shook his head.

"No—not yet, anyway."

McGurk looked up. "How about if Officer Yoshimura gave one of her fighting cat squawls and—"

"Just a sec!" Wanda had thrust her head forward another few inches. "There's something written on his collar, and I'm just beginning to make it out."

"Sure—the Williamses' phone number," said McGurk. "What are you wasting time over *that* for?"

"Because," said Wanda, as she peered at the collar, "it *isn't* the Williamses' number. It says 'Tiger.' And the name in front of the number is—uh—Russ—no—Russo."

"I guess it isn't Whiskers, then," said Willie. "I was beginning to think there was something wrong with my nose."

"Well—" McGurk began.

Then a voice behind us said:

"What do you kids think you're doing?"

We spun around. The speaker was a tall young man, wearing shorts and a headband. He looked as if he'd been jogging.

"Sir?"

For once, McGurk seemed lost for words.

"What are you doing with that cat?" demanded the man. He glanced at the tote bag. "Or *intending* to do?"

"It's a case of mistaken identity, sir," said McGurk. "We thought—"

"What's your name?" snapped the man. "I want *all* your names."

"We—we're on a *case*, sir," said McGurk. "My name's McGurk, head of the McGurk Organization. These are my officers. This is my ID."

The man frowned down at the ID card. Even with my typing, it looked—well—very homemade. The man studied it, took a deep breath, and said, "My name is Russo, John Russo, and that's my cat Tiger."

He still looked suspicious. "What kind of a case is it that makes you chase innocent cats up trees?" he asked.

"A missing person case, sir," said McGurk.

"Missing *what*?"

"Well—cat—sir," said McGurk.

"This one, sir," I said, showing him my notebook, opened at the relevant page.

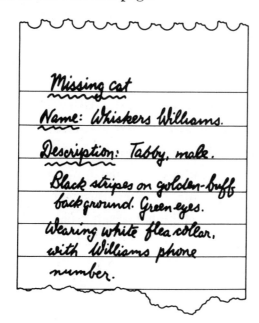

Missing cat
Name: Whiskers Williams.
Description: Tabby, male.
Black stripes on golden-buff
background. Green eyes.
Wearing white flea collar,
with Williams phone
number.

At last the man seemed convinced. He turned to McGurk.

"I thought you were trying to steal him," he said. "Sorry. But it did look suspicious."

"That's okay, sir," said McGurk. "Like I said—it was a case of mistaken identity." He hesitated. "But I don't think real cat thieves would operate in broad daylight."

"No, well," said Mr. Russo, "I guess it's a touchy subject around this neighborhood. Three cats have disappeared in the past four or five days."

"So the cat rustlers really have started to work this area?" said McGurk, giving us all a significant look. "Hear that, men?"

"Sure looks like it," said Mr. Russo. He was staring up at Tiger, all set to coax him down, probably.

Then McGurk had an afterthought. Giving the man a very keen look, he said, "Uh—how long have you owned Tiger, sir?"

"Why, ever since he was a kitten. He—" Suddenly, John Russo switched his stare from the cat to McGurk. "Hey, come on! You don't think *I* stole Whiskers and put a new collar on him, do you?"

McGurk relaxed his stern accusing expression. The cat was stretching himself, relaxing *his* stern expression.

"Well, no, sir. But you can't be too careful."

"Amen to that!" said the young man, as Tiger put out a paw, testing the trunk before beginning the climb down. "Anyway, you'd better go now, or you'll be making him nervous again. Good luck with Whiskers. . . ."

Two blocks away and about twenty minutes later, we thought the young man's wish had worked.

We'd been searching in the long, dry grass of a vacant lot. There were some ragged bushes there and heaps of builders' rubble. It looked as if there had once been a house on the spot—a house that had burned down, maybe, with the site only partially cleared. We'd been interested in a stack of rusty metal pipes—drainpipes wide enough for a cat to crawl in and out of. Mari had just bent to the opening of one of these and given one of her most plaintive cat wails.

And the response was like an echo. A deep and fruity warbling wail, but somehow thinner and more distant.

For a second or two I thought it was some trick of the sound waves as they went barreling through that pipe and out the other end.

Except that the response wasn't coming from that direction. It was coming from a shed at the end of the backyard of the house next door.

7 Pet Finders Inc.

"Did you hear that?" asked McGurk.

We were all looking toward the shed.

"It seemed to come from over there," I murmured.

"Officer Yoshimura," said McGurk. "One more time. The same sound."

Mari obliged.

There were a couple of seconds of silence. Then the warbling, gargling wail again. And this time there was no doubt. It came from that shed.

"Come on, men," said McGurk.

There was no fence around the yard next door. A few of the bushes looked as if they might have been the remains of a hedge. Otherwise, the only indication of a property line was that the grass on the house side was shorter and less untidy. Not a lot less untidy, though. In fact this line was so indistinct that no one could have been blamed for thinking the shed was actually *on* the vacant lot.

Anyway, here's a plan of the area:

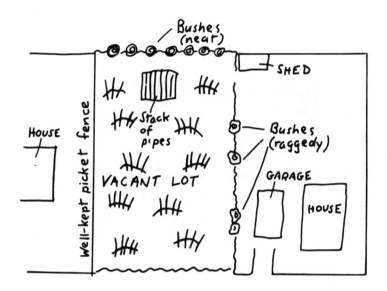

As we approached the shed, the door opened and a youth of about eighteen or nineteen stepped out. He frowned and stood between us and the shed, his feet planted firmly apart. He was wearing a short gray windbreaker and his hands were stuffed into the pockets with his elbows jutting out. It was as if he were saying, "Just try and get past me!"

What he did say was, "What d'ya want?"

He wasn't very tall, but he was stocky and powerful looking. He had a broad mouth that made him seem to be smiling, until you saw those frowning, unfriendly brown eyes. His skin was sallow, and there were blackheads on his lumpy nose.

"We heard a cat," said McGurk. "From in there."

"So?" said the youth, stiffening slightly.

"We're looking for a cat that strayed," said McGurk. "We thought it might have been shut in the shed accidentally."

"What kind of cat?"

"A tabby. Black stripes and—"

McGurk broke off at the sound of another squawling noise from the shed. I glanced at Mari, but her lips were shut tight as the squawling continued.

The youth turned. "Okay, Jamie," he said. "It's only a bunch of kids. Bring the cat and we'll get on with the job."

The door opened slowly, and the second youth appeared. He was taller than the other guy, but younger and thinner and softer looking. He had fair, floppy hair and what looked like a genuine smile but sort of weak and slack.

The most striking thing about him, though, was what he was carrying as he stepped out.

A cat basket. One of those with a plastic top. The cat inside wailed again as he approached us.

"Is *this* it?" sneered the older youth.

It was a Siamese.

"What are they looking for?" asked the other youth, his smile faltering a little.

"Some lousy old tabby," said the older one.

"He is *not* lousy!" said Wanda. "And he is *not* old!"

The older youth's sneer broadened. "Yours?" he asked.

"No," said McGurk, answering for Wanda. "It belongs to a friend. Ray Williams."

"Oh—*him!*" said the younger one.

"You know him?" said McGurk.

"Yeah," said Jamie. "He asked us to look for his cat, late Friday afternoon. But when we stopped by at his house to get all the details, he said he wouldn't pay our fee. So—" Jamie shrugged. "Tough!"

McGurk's eyes were just slits by now.

"Fee?"

"Yeah," said the older one. "A pet-finders' fee. We specialize in looking for lost pets."

"Pet Finders Incorporated," said Jamie. "That's us. Jamie Tait and Len Copeland. Right, Len?"

"Uh-huh," grunted Len, his brown eyes glittering back at McGurk's green ones. "Maybe you've seen our ad on the supermarket bulletin board. It—"

He broke off. A sleek Mercury had pulled up in the street.

"Here's Sheba's owner now," said Jamie.

Without another word, they both strolled over to the car, where the woman driver was getting out.

"I just couldn't wait!" she sang. "When I got your call I just couldn't wait even another ten minutes. . . . *Sheba, darling!*" she cried, as she bent to the carrier. "Mama's missed you terribly, terribly!"

Jamie handed her the carrier. Its inmate was wailing again, mingling her cries with the owner's.

"Oh, thank you, thank you, thank you, boys! I just can't thank you enough!"

Len Copeland said something in a low voice, as she placed the wailing carrier on the passenger seat.

"Of course!" said the woman, digging into her purse. "Right here!"

She handed over some bills to the older youth.

As the car drove off, Len Copeland's mouth really did smile for a few seconds.

"Another satisfied customer!" he said. Then, when he turned and saw us, the smile vanished. "You still here?" he grunted.

"Yes," said McGurk. "Have you *seen* anything of a cat that looks lost—one with black stripes on a brownish gray—"

"Lotsa times," said Len. "They're a dime a dozen. Now beat it. We're busy." He turned to his companion. "We have to look for that box turtle next, Jamie."

We resumed our search in thoughtful silence. It didn't take us long to be through with that area. And there was still no sign of Whiskers.

"By the way, Officer Sandowsky," said McGurk as we made our way back, passing the vacant lot once more, "did you happen to get a whiff of lavender when we were near the shed?"

"No," said Willie. "Only—"

"What's on your mind, McGurk?" said Wanda. "You heard what they said. They only deal in expensive pets."

McGurk shrugged. "Well, you never know." He turned to Willie. "Were you going to say something else?"

"Well," said Willie. "Only that I did get a whiff of catnip."

"I did, too," said Brains. "I guessed they'd have used it when they went looking for the Siamese."

"Yeah," murmured McGurk. "Maybe we should carry some ourselves when we go looking for Whiskers tomorrow."

"It's overrated, in my opinion," said Brains. "Mari's cat calls are ten times more powerful, I bet."

McGurk seemed to cheer up. I think he'd been finding it hard to take: the fact that there was another, apparently more successful organization at work.

"*I gotta get out of here!*"

The sudden cry from around the back of Mrs. Berg's made McGurk realize where we were.

"We'll just have a word with Ray Williams if he's in," he said.

Ray was in. His face fell when he saw that Wanda's tote bag was empty.

"We hear you asked some other guys to search for Whiskers," said McGurk, in a voice that was both hurt and accusing. "Before coming to us."

"Yeah!" said Ray, indignantly. "Those creeps! Pet Finders Inc., they call themselves. Making out to be specialists!"

"They said you didn't want to pay their fee," said McGurk, in the same dark tone.

"Didn't *want* to?" said Ray. "*Couldn't* is more like it. You know what they were asking?"

We shook our heads.

"They were asking five dollars up front! Five dollars!" Ray's voice was full of anguish. "And another ten if and when they delivered him!"

"Wow!" gasped Willie. "Who can pay that kind of money?"

"*I* can't, for one!" said Ray.

"The woman with the Siamese could, though," said Wanda.

"What Siamese?" asked Ray.

We told him about Sheba and her owner.

Ray nodded.

"That's what bugs me," he said bitterly. "They *are* good. I mean that's the second Siamese they've found in the past week. Plus a Burmese *and* a Russian Blue. Why—that's sixty dollars!"

"Who *said* they'd found these other three?" asked McGurk.

"They did," said Ray.

"Oh—*them!*" said McGurk. "That would be just sales talk. Anyway, it's time we packed in for the day now."

"You'll still be looking for Whiskers tomorrow, though?" asked Ray, suddenly anxious.

"Don't worry," said McGurk. "We will. What's more, we'll find him—if—if it takes us a month. I mean anyone can find some flashy-looking Siamese, but it takes real detectives to track down a tabby with a million look-alikes."

"Well . . . I hope so," murmured Ray.

"And it won't cost you an arm and a leg, either," said McGurk.

I had never seen him look so determined. And,

as if to underline this, he said to me before we split up for the night: "First thing in the morning, Officer Rockaway, I want you to stop by at the supermarket and make a copy of that Pet Finders ad."

I grinned.

"Nothing like checking out the competition, huh, McGurk?"

He managed a faint smile, but his overall expression was very preoccupied.

"Something like that . . ." he said.

8 The Unfaithful Client

McGurk was still in a subdued mood the following morning. I was a few minutes late. The others were sitting at their places around the table. McGurk didn't comment on my lateness. Instead, he just said quietly, "Sit down, Officer Rockaway." Then he turned to the others and said, "Where was I?"

"You'd just been asking if any of us knew who some lady was," said Brains.

"Only you didn't say which lady," said Willie.

"If you meant the lady who came to collect her Siamese cat—" Wanda began.

"Yes," said McGurk, impatiently. "Who else?"

"Well, I know who she is," said Wanda. "She's called Mrs. Cranshaw, and she lives not far from us."

"Good," said McGurk, beginning to rock slightly. "We'll have a word with her later."

"What about?" said Brains.

McGurk didn't seem to hear him.

"Well, Officer Rockaway?" he said. "Did you collect the information?"

"Sure thing," I replied, opening my notebook.

He bent over it, frowning.

Here is what I'd collected:

Exact copy, Pet Finders'
ad. on supermarket
bulletin board:

PET FINDERS INC.
Let us find your lost
pet. Cats, dogs, gerbils,
etc. etc.
Reasonible (sic)
fees. Call 698 9350

"Is that it?" McGurk said.

"Yes," I said. "Handwritten, on a postcard."

"What's this about being sick?" he asked.

"That's what I put in. *Sic*, without a *k*. It means that that's exactly how they'd misspelled 'reasonable.' Their mistake, not mine. It's a Latin word meaning—"

"All right, all right!" growled McGurk. "We're not here for a Latin lesson."

"I should hope not," said Wanda. "A lovely morning like this."

She'd brought along the tote bag again and looked eager to resume the search.

McGurk sighed and stood up.

"Okay, men," he said. "We'll carry on where we left off and cover the next area to the north."

"Good!" said Brains, looking pleased—no doubt because we were still sticking with his theory. "I've got a feeling we'll find him today."

"I wish *I* had," said McGurk. "All set, Officer Yoshimura?"

"Meow!" said Mari.

"Me, too," said Willie. "If there's any lavender smell out there—"

"Sure," said McGurk, wearily. "So save your breath and give your nose a chance, Officer Sandowsky."

On the way out, we looked at each other with raised eyebrows. It was very rare for McGurk not to be gung ho on a job like this.

To get to the next unsearched area to the north, we had to go past the vacant lot. I mean we didn't *have* to—we could have gone along any of the north-south avenues—but that was the way McGurk led us.

And, as we approached the spot, McGurk's face brightened up.

"Looks like they've got company, men," he said. "Slow down a little."

There was an old empty pickup truck parked beside the lot. The driver was on the sidewalk, talking to Tait and Copeland. He was a short, stocky barrel of a man with a greasy face and a few days' growth of black stubble on his chin. And although he was talking in a low voice, hoarse and rasping, we could tell from its tone that he was giving the two guys a piece of his mind.

"Anyways," he grunted, giving us a quick, shifty look from his little glittering skunklike eyes as we drew alongside, "remember! No more goofing off. Okay?"

We continued to walk past.

"Did I hear a cat down at the other end of the vacant lot again?" said McGurk, in a fairly loud voice. And, without waiting for a reply, he said, "Come on, men! We'll just take another look."

As we walked through the long grass, the man got back into his truck and started the engine with a roaring rasp. It was probably a faulty muffler, but it sounded like one last angry reminder to Tait and Copeland.

No more goofing off from *what*? I wondered.

"Anyone recognize the guy?" McGurk asked, making a pretense of looking through one of the stacked pipes.

"Yes," said Brains. "I did."

McGurk straightened up, face flushed, eyes gleaming.

"You sure, Officer Bellingham?"

"Positive!" said Brains. "His name's Jeb Lee. He lives in an old trailer home near Brackman's Swamp. His yard's full of all sorts of old junk, mainly cars. Looks like a cemetery for old jalopies. He's got more in his barn, too."

"How d'you know all this?" asked McGurk.

"My dad took me there," said Brains. "When he was looking for a spare part for our old—"

"What do you jerks want *this* time?" a voice broke in. "Still looking for the Williams cat?"

It was Len Copeland. He and his sidekick had come level with us, pausing at the door of the shed.

"Yes," said McGurk. "Seen anything of him?"

His eyes were so keen and fierce as he looked from Copeland's face to Tait's that the latter blinked and looked down.

Copeland continued to stare right back, however.

"No, we haven't," he said. "And I don't think we'd bother telling *you* if we had."

"Oh?" said McGurk.

"No," said Copeland. Suddenly he grinned. "After all, you *are* in business as detectives, aren't you?"

"Yes," said McGurk, sticking out his chest. "And we're very good at it, too!"

"Sure," said Copeland. "That's what we heard. So do your own searching. Only I'll give you a tip."

"About Whiskers?" said McGurk.

"No," said Copeland. "About you. All of you. Stick to investigating burglaries and stuff like that."

"I mean, you can look for some cheapskate's old tabby cat all you want," said Jamie Tait. "But real professional pet finding is now *our* territory."

"Exclusively!" said Copeland.

McGurk stuck out his chest again.

"Pet finding!" he said. "Penny-ante stuff! It's only because Ray—"

"Talking about penny-ante stuff," sneered Len Copeland, "Ray Williams called us up this morning saying he was now ready to pay us after all. Right, Jamie?"

Jamie snickered. "Right!" he said. "Only we told him nothing doing, we're all booked up."

"So get lost!" said Copeland. "We're busy."

As we continued on our way north to the next search area, McGurk was strangely silent. His face had turned from red to white when he'd heard about Ray offering to hire Pet Finders Inc., after all. I guessed it was the shock and the feeling of being somehow betrayed.

Anyway, after we'd searched the new area—without any success—we went back to our own neighborhood.

"Before we split up for lunch, men," said McGurk, with a glint in his eyes, "we'll have a word with Ray Williams."

"Our faithful client!" said Wanda bitterly.

"*I gotta get out of here!*" Ziggy was yelling, as we walked up the Williamses' driveway.

"So you decided to hire Pet Finders after all?" said McGurk when Ray came to the door.

"You heard about that, then?" mumbled Ray.

"Yes," said Wanda. "And we think you have a nerve, after everything we've—"

"Be quiet, Officer Grieg!" said McGurk. "The client has a right to hire whoever he wants."

"Gee, thanks, McGurk!" said Ray. "I knew you'd understand. I mean, I wasn't asking them to search *instead* of you. I was thinking *as well as,* and—"

"Sure," said McGurk. "But"—his frown deepened—"is it true they refused to handle the case? Did you haggle over the fee, or what?"

"No, no! I offered them the full fifteen dollars.

I'd managed to scrape the money together—but—" Ray shrugged. "They—they just weren't interested anymore."

"You sure love that cat, don't you?" said Wanda, no longer looking mad at Ray.

Ray nodded, his face miserable.

McGurk was looking thoughtful again. Very thoughtful and very grave.

"Don't worry, Ray," he murmured. "*We're* still on the case."

"You think—you think you'll find him?" stammered Ray.

"We'll do our best," said McGurk.

His face didn't have much expression at all, but knowing McGurk as well as I do I could tell that he wasn't feeling anything like as confident about finding Whiskers as he'd been earlier.

In fact, if I'd been updating his shield, this is how it would have looked:

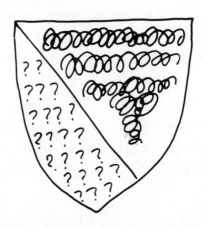

With thick smoke instead of fire, and question marks instead of freckles.

The Knight of the Fiery Freckles had become the Knight of the Smoldering Questions.

McGurk Sees a Pattern

After lunch, McGurk announced that he was changing our tactics.

"We've given Officer Bellingham's theory a fair trial," he said, "but we can't keep *on* going north when the cat might be somewhere in any of the other three directions. Okay?"

We all agreed, except Brains.

"It's very unscientific, McGurk," he said. "I mean when you have a theory you have to stick with it until—"

"Sorry, Officer Bellingham!" said McGurk. "Theories are theories and hunches are hunches. And *my* hunch right now is to search at random. Plus, at the same time, to check up on those Pet Finders creeps. Where did you say the lady with the Siamese lives, Officer Grieg?"

Wanda told him, and we went to see Mrs. Cranshaw.

"What do you suspect, McGurk?" I asked as we approached the house.

"I'm not sure," he growled. "Yet."

I guessed it was just his professional jealousy and that he was hoping to find the reports of our rivals' success to be grossly exaggerated. If so, he was in for a big disappointment.

"I can't recommend them too highly," said Mrs. Cranshaw. She was a thin, delicate-looking woman with very big brown eyes. Those eyes had begun to glow as soon as McGurk mentioned Pet Finders Inc. "Why do you ask?"

"We're looking for a cat, ma'am," said McGurk. "It's been missing since Wednesday."

The woman's eyes became instantly bright and moist.

"Oh, dear!" she said. "That was two days before Sheba disappeared." She bent down and picked up the Siamese, which had come to the door with her. Hugging the cat, she said, "Sheba disappeared around ten o'clock on Friday evening. And those two young men had her back home by two-thirty on Sunday afternoon. She was missing for less than forty-eight hours, weren't you, honey?"

The cat touched her nose with its own.

"There, you see!" said the woman. "She says yes."

I wondered what the cat would have to say if it

could *really* talk. But McGurk seemed satisfied with the plain human answers he was getting from the owner.

"How did you know about Pet Finders, ma'am? Their ad in the supermarket?"

"Oh, no!" said Mrs. Cranshaw. "I didn't even know they existed. They came to me on Saturday afternoon, offering their services. They said they'd heard about our problem."

"So you were very pleased with their service, ma'am?"

"I surely am," said the woman, smiling at Mari, who was gently tickling the cat under its chin. "Their fee was rather high, but it was worth every cent. But don't just take my word for it. Ask Mrs. Taylor. They found her Natasha just as quickly."

She gave us this other woman's address.

McGurk thanked her.

Mrs. Cranshaw held Sheba's paw out to wave good-bye as we went down the driveway.

"I hope you were getting all that down, Officer Rockaway?" said McGurk, with a pleased glint in his eyes.

"Yes, of course," I said. "Look."

I showed him where I had roughly scribbled down the facts as related by Mrs. Cranshaw—mainly the times and the days.

"Good work, Officer Rockaway!" he said. "Keep it up. I want to see what kind of pattern there is to this"—his lip curled—"this *success* story!"

He interviewed four more pet owners during the next couple of hours. All of them had cause to recommend our new rivals, and all of them were willing to pass on the names of other satisfied clients. Later, he had me type out the results in a neat table— which I now reproduce here:

PET	TIME WHEN FIRST MISSED	TIME WHEN P.F.I. OFFERED TO SEARCH	TIME WHEN FOUND
Cat, Siamese, "Sheba"	Friday, 10 p.m.	Saturday, 3:30 p.m.	Sunday, 2:30 p.m.
Cat, Russian Blue, "Natasha"	Wednesday, 9:30 p.m.	Thursday, 5:00 p.m.	Friday, 10:00 a.m.
Cat, Burmese, "Tun Tin"	Thursday, 8:30 p.m.	Friday, 11:30 a.m.	Saturday, 11:00 a.m.
Cat, Siamese, "Lotus Petal"	Tuesday, 10:00 p.m.	Wednesday, 9:30 a.m.	Wednesday, 2:30 p.m.
Turtle, Box, "Billy"	Saturday, 8:30 a.m.	Sunday, 11:00 a.m.	Sunday, 5:30 p.m.

Set out like that, the pattern is fairly clear; but even when the facts were only in rough note form, it was becoming clear enough. Especially to McGurk.

"I mean, come on!" he said, after the last interview. "Four cats. All disappearing in the dark. All returned in less than a couple of days. All the owners approached by those creeps the following day. I mean they weren't leaving it to chance, were they? They weren't leaving it for the owners to see the ad in the supermarket and approach *them*?"

"You think they stole the pets, McGurk?" said Willie.

"Well, *borrowed* them, yes," said McGurk. "Borrowed them for a night or two. Before returning them for a fat fee. Probably the cat rustler scare gave them the idea."

"What about Whiskers, then," said Wanda. "Do you think they borrowed *him*?"

McGurk frowned.

"I'm not sure," he said. "Probably not. Probably Whiskers really did go astray, and the creeps got to hear of it and decided to cash in on their reputation by conning Ray out of a down payment." He shook his head. He looked very gloomy again. "I don't know."

"Should I go on making my cat noises, Chief McGurk?" said Mari.

McGurk shrugged.

"Sure," he said, forcing a grin. "We haven't given up on Whiskers yet. No way!"

As Mari went into one of her feline wails, seeming to put into it all the gloom and doom that had quickly come back to McGurk's face, Wanda turned to him.

"What's wrong, McGurk?" she asked quietly. "I mean you don't really sound very confident. *Are* you giving up on Whiskers, or what?"

McGurk shrugged again.

"Well," he said, "maybe we'll *have* to give up on him."

"Why?" asked Wanda.

"I've got an uneasy feeling that he's miles away by now," he said. "Maybe in New York City."

Wanda looked horrified. We all did.

"Rustlers?" she whispered.

"Yeah," said McGurk. "I—"

We'd been speaking in low voices because by now we were at the corner of the street on which Ray lives, and you never know. The possibility that Whiskers had been stolen by the rustlers was bad enough for *us* to digest. It would have to be broken to Ray very gently.

But McGurk hadn't broken off because he'd just caught sight of Ray.

It was because Mrs. Berg had just come flying out of her driveway crying, "Oh! Oh! Thank goodness you're there! Come quickly, please, come quickly! Ziggy's disappeared!"

10 Patrolman Cassidy Stops By

I thought at first that Mrs. Berg had flipped. As we followed her to the back of the house, I heard distinctly the yell: *"How* dare *you talk to me like that!"*

But when we turned the corner I could see that the voice was coming from the small radio on the porch table, not from the cage. The cage wasn't there.

"Where's the cage, ma'am?" asked McGurk.

"They took that, too!" said Mrs. Berg. Her usually smooth face was all puckered up and twitching. "Oh, dear!" she moaned. "I do hope they'll be able to find him!"

" 'They,' ma'am?" asked McGurk.

"The police," said Mrs. Berg. "Or—or—*you—anybody!"*

"Have you called the police, ma'am?"

"Yes," said Mrs. Berg, her eyes roving around, as if she expected to see Ziggy flying over the backyard at any moment. "They said they'd come right away. I was looking out for them when I saw you."

"Come away from the porch, men," said McGurk, stepping down onto the grass.

We followed him.

"When did you discover he was gone, Mrs. Berg?" asked Wanda.

"As soon as I got back from the supermarket," said Mrs. Berg.

"Supermarket?" asked McGurk, frowning.

"Yes," she said. "I'd gone down to the supermarket to get a few things I'd run short of. I wasn't away for more than half an hour."

McGurk's frown deepened.

"Break-ins and thefts usually take a lot less time than that, ma'am," he said, glancing around the porch.

Mrs. Berg's cheeks were turning red.

"Yes—well—anyway—it seemed such a shame to disturb him," she said. "So I left him out on the porch listening to his favorite talk show. I did hang the cage up from the roof, out of the way of cats."

She switched off the radio.

"Funnily enough," she went on, "I'd just been thinking how safe he was, compared to other pets. Like Ray's cat, for instance. I'd stopped in front of the bulletin board before getting my groceries, and the two young men who call themselves Pet Finders were there."

"Oh?" said McGurk.

"Yes. They were with a member of the office staff," said Mrs. Berg. "They were making some additions to their notice. And I said to myself then, 'Well, Sylvia Berg, there's no risk of *your* pet going astray.'" She sighed. "It just shows you."

"What additions were they making?" I asked.

"Oh, about how they had a one-hundred-percent track record," said Mrs. Berg. "Five cats, a gerbil, a box turtle."

I couldn't help grinning slightly. It sounded just like the way McGurk is always adding to *our* notice.

"Well, this is out of their league now," he said, with a gleam of what looked like satisfaction in his eyes. "Are those his feathers, ma'am?" He pointed to the floor, where two or three small blue-gray feathers lay.

Mrs. Berg peered at them.

"Why, yes!" she said. "They must have fallen—"

"No! Don't touch them!" snapped McGurk.

"Leave everything just as is, until the police come."

"Poor lamb!" said Mrs. Berg, still staring at the feathers as she straightened up. "He must have gotten so excited and upset when they were taking his cage down!"

Brains cleared his throat.

"Where's that from, Mrs. Berg?" he asked, pointing to something shiny near the edge of the porch steps. "That split pin."

I made a rough sketch of it at the time. Here it is:

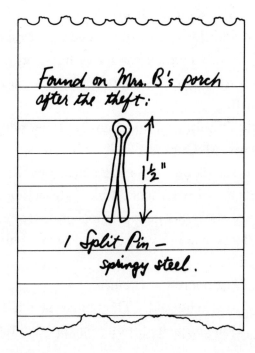

"Oh, that," said Mrs. Berg, stooping.

"Don't touch it, ma'am!" McGurk snapped.

"It must have dropped off the cage," said Mrs. Berg.

"Oh?" said McGurk.

"Yes," she said. "I put it at the end of the bolt on his door, after I've slid it shut."

"Ma'am?"

"I clip it on one of the bars at that point," said Mrs. Berg. "So that even if Ziggy gets hold of the end of the bolt he can't slide it open. He's gotten very clever at that. He—oh, I think they're here!"

There'd been the sound of a car door being slammed shut, followed by heavy footsteps.

It was Patrolman Cassidy, the elderly cop who's a special friend of ours.

"Well, well, well, M'Quirk!" he said. "You beat us to it this time!"

(It's an old joke of his to pretend to forget McGurk's real name.)

"Yes, sir," said McGurk. "I've had my officers keep off the porch."

Patrolman Cassidy fingered his grizzled mustache and nodded. Then he turned to Mrs. Berg.

"I hear you lost a canary, ma'am?"

"A parrot, officer," said Mrs. Berg. "A very valuable parrot. Worth almost two thousand dollars."

Mr. Cassidy gave a low whistle.

"Where was it?" he asked. "Out here?"

"Yes. In his cage," said Mrs. Berg.

"Did they take the cage, too?" the cop asked, looking up from his notes.

"Yes," said Mrs. Berg.

"How much was *that* worth?" asked Mr. Cassidy.

"I don't know offhand," said Mrs. Berg. "It came with the parrot." Her voice broke a little. "My— my children bought me the parrot for Christmas."

"Where were you, ma'am?" the cop asked. "When this happened?"

"I'd just gone down to the supermarket. It couldn't have been for more than half an hour."

"Most household break-ins take a lot less time than that, ma'am," said Mr. Cassidy.

McGurk's face was radiant. "That's what I was telling Mrs. Berg," he said. "Just a few minutes ago."

"Well, you're right, M'Turk." The cop gave his mustache another stroke as he looked at us. "Where were *you?*"

"We were on another case, sir," said McGurk. "Making inquiries about a missing cat."

"Oh, that . . ." said Mr. Cassidy. "Yeah. It's get-

ting to be an epidemic. So far eleven have disappeared in the last seven days. To *our* knowledge."

"That pin came off the cage, Mr. Cassidy," said
Brains.

"Which pin?" said the cop, looking down.

"You're standing on it, sir," said Brains.

Mrs. Berg explained about it as Mr. Cassidy
picked it up and examined it.

"Hm!" said the cop, thoughtfully. "Pretty strong
clip. It wouldn't just fall off—it would need *pulling*
off. It looks like they were intending to open the
door and just grab the bird."

"Oh, but they'd never be able to handle Ziggy
that way!" said Mrs. Berg.

"No, ma'am," said Mr. Cassidy. "All I mean is
that they probably didn't figure on taking the cage,
at first. Not until they realized they had to."

Wanda was looking puzzled. "They'd be very con-
spicuous, though, wouldn't they? Carrying a big
cage."

"Not if they'd come in a car and driven up alongside," said Mr. Cassidy. He turned to Mrs. Berg.
"Anyway, ma'am, we'll ask around, see if anyone
noticed a car in your driveway. Also pet stores. See
if anyone's been trying to peddle a parrot."

"And don't forget the hospital, sir," said Brains,

glancing at the finger that Ziggy had pecked. "And local physicians. To see if anyone checks in with parrot bites."

"Good thinking, young man!" said Mr. Cassidy, making a note of it and causing Brains's face to glow.

But McGurk wasn't going to be outshone by one of his officers.

"What if it was only the cage they were after, sir?" he said. "Might they have just let the bird loose, not knowing how valuable he was?"

Mrs. Berg gave a little gasp. Mr. Cassidy nodded.

"It's an idea, McGurk," he said. "We'll ask around about that, too. Anyone seeing a parrot flying around." He turned to Mrs. Berg. "What kind was— is—it, ma'am?"

"An African Gray," she said.

"About sixteen inches long," I said, reading from my notebook. "About the size of a crow. With light blue-gray feathers, lighter on the head, red feathers under its tail, and black feet."

It gave me a kick seeing Patrolman Cassidy writing these details down in *his* notebook.

"I guess you guys will be able to help there?" he asked. "On the lookout for an escaped parrot?"

"Sure thing!" said McGurk.

"And—and maybe I'll ask Pet Finders Incorporated," said Mrs. Berg. "Just to leave no stone unturned."

"Who're they?" asked Mr. Cassidy.

"Oh, just a rival organization," said McGurk, giving Mrs. Berg a quick frown.

Patrolman Cassidy put the notebook back in his pocket. "Getting some competition, huh, McKirk? Nothing like it for keeping you on your toes."

"No, sir," said McGurk, giving us *all* a frown.

After Mr. Cassidy had gone, Mrs. Berg turned to McGurk. "Oh, you *will* look out for him, won't you? If—if they did let Ziggy loose? If it *was* only his cage they wanted?"

"Sure," said McGurk. His frown had deepened. "But I doubt it."

"What?" asked Mrs. Berg. "You doubt what?"

"That it was only the cage they wanted," he said. "I've been having second thoughts about that."

For a moment I thought McGurk was only saying this to pay her back for saying she might hire the Pet Finders. But he had a much better reason.

"If they'd only wanted the cage," he said, "not realizing Ziggy's value, they'd probably have taken that, too." He nodded toward the radio.

Mrs. Berg's face fell.

"Oh, yes—of course . . ." she murmured. Then

she looked up, startled. "Oh, we didn't tell Mr. Cassidy about the things Ziggy says! They'll be the best identification of all. I must call him and tell him."

"Yes, ma'am," said McGurk. "Uh—how long does that talk show go on?"

He asked the question brightly. His eyes now had that certain gleam in them. Uh-oh, I thought. What's he coming up with now?

"Which show?" asked Mrs. Berg, looking a little confused.

"The one that Ziggy likes," he said.

"Oh, that!" she said. "Until six."

"What time is it now?" McGurk asked Brains, who was already looking at his huge wristwatch.

"4:06 exactly," said our science expert. "In London it's 9:06 and in Tokyo—"

"Just the regular time, Officer Bellingham." McGurk turned to Mrs. Berg. "What station, ma'am?" he asked. Then, turning to me: "Officer Rockaway, take this down."

Puzzled, I made a note as Mrs. Berg gave us the number.

"Fine!" said McGurk, reaching out for my book and tearing out the page with the number on it. "Okay, Officer Yoshimura," he said, handing Mari the page. "I want you to go home right now, turn that program on and listen carefully—especially when the guy says any of the things that Ziggy says."

Mari's eyes glowed. "You bet, Chief McGurk!"

"Then report to HQ at five o'clock and we'll take it from there," said McGurk. As Mari sped off, McGurk turned. "The rest of us," he said, "will be asking around just in case anyone *has* seen the bird flying loose. If it is, it could still be close to here."

This galvanized Mrs. Berg.

"Oh—then let me show you how to recapture him," she said. "And what with," she added, hurrying off indoors.

11 Inside the Shed

We spent the next fifty minutes going around the immediate neighborhood with a towel, a fishing net, and a small carrying cage.

The idea was to net the bird from behind, swinging the net in the same direction as he was flying—then quickly putting the towel in front of the net's opening.

"Then you put the net—still with the towel over it—in front of the cage's open door and quickly slip the towel away," Mrs. Berg had explained.

Well, that was okay if the bird was flying around indoors, I guess.

And it might have been okay even outdoors, if Ziggy had been anywhere within reach.

But the nearest we got was when we asked a bunch of little kids if they'd seen a big bluish-gray bird flying around.

"Oh, yeah, sure," said one of them.

"One that was making a big screeching sound?" asked McGurk.

"Yeah! Yeah!" they all chorused. "Up there! In that tree!"

It was one of the trees lining the avenue. It had more leaves than the one Wanda had climbed when we were looking for Whiskers, and we couldn't see beyond the lowest limbs.

"Officer Grieg . . ." McGurk said quietly, handing her the fishing net.

"I can't do all that up *there!*" Wanda protested. "I need my hands for climbing!"

"Okay," said McGurk, grudgingly. "So scare him down then. Officer Rockaway, you get ready with the towel. Officer Sandowsky, have the cage ready."

Wanda was already up and out of sight, except for her feet.

"See anything of him?" McGurk asked.

There was no answer, just a grunt. Then suddenly there was a very loud shattering screech. I tightened my grip on the towel.

"It's there!" said one of the kids, as the blue and white bird came flashing out.

"That's a blue jay!" said McGurk, scowling at the kids.

"Yeah!" said one of them. "Aren't you gonna catch him?"

"Is that the one you meant?" Wanda asked, as she lowered herself to the ground.

"Yeah! Yeah!" said the last kid. "These dummies just missed him!"

By the time we'd returned to our HQ, the jay was the only sighting we'd heard of.

"It looks like zilch for Ziggy," said Wanda.

"Yeah, well, it was only an outside chance," said McGurk. He kept glancing impatiently at the door. It was five past five already. "Where's Officer Yoshimura? What's keeping her?"

"It must be something important," said Wanda. "It isn't like Mari to be late."

But it was 5:15 by the time Mari arrived, and McGurk was fit to be tied.

"Come on, Officer Yoshimura!" he growled. "You're holding us all up!"

"Sorry, Chief McGurk," she said. "I—"

"Did you listen to the guy carefully, like I said?"

"Yes, Chief McGurk. I am very sorry. But he was so good. He could tell by voices of callers if they were lying. Very quickly. First few words. Just as I can."

McGurk's scowl deepened.

"I didn't ask you to listen just for your own special interest, Officer Yoshimura. I—"

"How dare *you talk to me like that!"*

The voice, high-pitched and vibrant with indignation, seemed to come from Willie. And I must say Willie had his mouth open. But it was with amazement.

McGurk had glared at him for a second or two, but then he turned back to Mari—amazed himself, and delighted, no longer scowling.

"You?" he said.

Mari smiled slightly. I swear that was the only movement of her lips. But from the bottom of our boxes of files in the corner, there had come this croak:

"I gotta get out of here!"

"Great!" said McGurk. "Good work, Officer Yoshimura! Now we are *really* fully equipped to go looking for Ziggy!"

As we headed north along Pine Avenue, armed with net, towel, carrying cage, and Mari's carrying voice, we stopped several times to let her try her luck.

In fact, I mentally changed her shield, which I later copied out for the record like this:

Her "How dare you talk to me . . ." was always the same, just like Ziggy's but slightly more human; but her "I gotta get out of here!" came in several versions. Sometimes it was a sad croak; sometimes it came out as a series of dying gasps; sometimes it sounded to be on the verge of tears; and sometimes it seemed to be on the verge of hysterical, broken-down laughter.

"But the man says it in all of these ways," she assured us. "That is why I stayed listening longer."

"You did good, Officer Yoshimura," McGurk said. "But from here on in, keep it under wraps until I give you the word."

"Here on in *where*?" asked Wanda.

"The Pet Finders jerks' shed," said McGurk. "We're only a couple of blocks away, and I don't want to give them any advance warning."

This was pretty good thinking on McGurk's part, because when we reached the vacant lot, Tait and Copeland were just coming from the direction of the house toward the shed.

They stopped when they saw us.

"Still looking for that old tabby cat?" Tait sneered.

"No," said McGurk. "A parrot."

I was surprised at McGurk coming straight out with it. But then I guessed he might as well have said it, seeing that Wanda was carrying the birdcage. I mean it was smaller than Ziggy's regular cage, but there was no way she could have concealed it behind her back.

Copeland didn't change his expression. He just stood there with his hands stuffed in his windbreaker pockets, staring at us blankly. Jamie Tait's smile did seem to waver, though, when McGurk mentioned the parrot.

"There's no parrot around here," said Tait, shrugging.

"It might still be in its cage," said McGurk, looking at them narrowly.

That brought a reply from Copeland. He blinked and said, "Who's lost one?"

"Mrs. Berg!" said Wanda, accusingly. "That's who!"

"Next door to Ray Williams?" said Jamie Tait.

A quiver of annoyance passed across Copeland's face as he gave Jamie a quick glance.

"Yes," said McGurk. "Do you know her?"

"I can't say we do," Copeland put in quickly. "But maybe we'll give her a buzz. See if she wants a couple of *real* pet finders on the job."

"Yeah!" said McGurk. "Why don't you do that?"

Suddenly, Copeland grinned.

"Hey, Jamie!" he said. "I think this guy suspects *us*!"

"Oh, yeah?" said Tait, grinning back, but more uncertainly.

"Yeah," said Copeland. "He keeps looking at the shed. I bet he thinks we've got the parrot in there."

"You—you don't say!" murmured Tait, now looking *very* uncertain.

Copeland's sneer widened. "So why don't we let them take a peek inside?"

"Yeah," said Tait, seeming to brighten up. "Why not?"

Copeland went and opened the shed door, inviting us to look inside with a jerk of the head. I for one was more interested in looking at his right hand just then. He'd taken it out of his pocket to open the door. It had four or five small patches on the back. Not regular *strips,* please note, such as he might have used for scratches. Just those small round ones, the size of a quarter.

Brains was studying them, too, but McGurk seemed more interested in looking inside the shed. I wondered about this, knowing he was smart enough to realize the parrot couldn't have been in there if Copeland had invited us to take a look.

But then I saw him turn and stand aside and tug at Willie's sleeve—and then I knew what he was *really* hoping for.

Anyway, there was no cage in there, no parrot. Just a couple of old tote bags, a spade, a rake, and some other odds and ends of junk.

"Don't you want to see *inside* the bags?" said Copeland. "I mean, do feel free."

As he spoke, he bent to the bags and unzippered them.

McGurk peered into the gaping openings, and again he tugged at Willie's sleeve, getting him to look, too.

Well—"look" isn't the right word, of course.

"Okay," said McGurk, when Willie had taken a few gentle sniffs. He turned to Copeland. "Sorry about that. There's no parrot here."

"No," said Copeland, looking ugly again, "so beat

it. You're beginning to annoy me!"

We got out of the shed pretty fast. The two jerks stayed inside. One of them slammed the door shut after us.

"Anything, Officer Sandowsky?" said McGurk as we crossed over into the vacant lot.

Willie was frowning.

"Mainly disinfectant," he said.

"That *all*?"

"Well," Willie's nose wrinkled slightly, "well, two things really."

"What two things?"

"Well, cats—there was a definite cat whiff."

"And?" McGurk urged.

"And—and lavender. Just a trace of it. Spike lavender."

McGurk had been leading the way through the long grass to the pile of drainpipes. We were now between the pipes and the bushes at the end of the lot, out of sight of anyone looking out the shed window, which faced the house and garage.

"Wow!" said Wanda. "It looks like Whiskers *was* in there at some time, after all!"

"Yeah," murmured McGurk, looking preoccupied. "Now get down, all of you, behind these pipes."

We crouched as ordered.

Then McGurk turned to Mari and said, "When I give the signal, Officer Yoshimura, I want you to throw your voice toward that garage and give out with the 'How dare you' bit. As loud and shrieky and as near to Ziggy's voice as you can make it!"

Mari nodded, her eyes already narrowing, her head already poised. Then McGurk dropped a hand on her shoulder and:

"*How* dare *you talk to me like that!*"

The words cut through the air above the pipes and grass, piercing the branches of one of the stunted bushes, and bounced off the garage's back wall.

"Now down, get down!" whispered McGurk.

There was silence for a second or two. Then the sound of the shed door being flung open and the thud of running footsteps.

I decided it was safe to raise my head. The two guys had their backs to us as they hurried toward the garage and rounded its corner.

Then came the rumbling sound of a garage door being lifted, silence again, and finally the starting of a car engine.

"And that's why they didn't mind us looking in the shed," said McGurk, as we watched the beat-up old Thunderbird turn into the avenue and speed away.

"Why?" said Willie.

"Because they knew they'd left the parrot in the garage," said Wanda. "Right, McGurk?"

"Right."

"So what happens now?" said Brains. "All we've done is get them to stash it someplace else."

"Sure," said McGurk. "Which is probably what they were going to do anyway."

"But *where*, McGurk?" I asked.

"I'm not sure," he murmured. "That's going to be our next step—*finding out* where."

12 The Suspects' Profiles

After we'd taken the net, the towel, and the carrying cage back to Mrs. Berg, McGurk said:

"Right, men! We'll meet up at eight-thirty sharp tomorrow morning. In the meantime, I want you to find out all you can about the suspects, Copeland and Tait. Especially you, Officer Grieg."

"Why me?" said Wanda.

"Because your brother Ed's a high-school senior and he's more likely to know them."

The rest of us didn't have that advantage. But there were still indirect lines of inquiry that could be followed. I for one followed them, anyway. How? By looking in the phone book.

There were two Copelands listed, but only one

had a local address, Pine Avenue. So that left three Taits, none of them in this neighborhood. Which was Jamie's address stumped me—though I had a strong hunch that it was the one on River Road. That neighborhood of closely huddled dilapidated houses somehow seemed to fit his general appearance.

Anyway, shortly after 8:30 the next morning, I discovered my hunch had been right. Wanda, as expected, turned up with the most details.

"Len Copeland," she said, "is nineteen. His parents are divorced, and he lives with his mother on Pine—in the house next to the vacant lot. His mother has two jobs: one as an office cleaner and another as a waitress at the Tip Top Diner. He dropped out of high school two years ago. He's never had any regular employment, even though there are plenty of jobs available."

"Are you getting this down, Officer Rockaway?" asked McGurk.

"Trying to," I said, scribbling away. "Okay, continue with the profile, Wanda."

"Profile . . ." said McGurk. "That's a good police word. Carry on with the profile, Officer Grieg."

"Thanks!" she said, with an impatient toss of her hair. "Well, Copeland's been in trouble with the

police more than once. Mainly petty thefts. Oh—
and driving that old Thunderbird without proper
insurance. He paid four hundred dollars for that
heap of junk, as Ed calls it. About a year ago."

"How do you know the price?" asked McGurk.

"Because Ed was interested in buying it, too.
Until he saw it."

"Who from?" said Brains.

"Ed didn't give any name," said Wanda. "Just that
it was somewhere on the outskirts of town. He mentioned the place but—"

"But it's irrelevant!" said McGurk, scowling at
Brains. "Go on, Officer Grieg—what else do you
have?"

"Nothing more about Copeland," said Wanda.
"And not a whole lot about Jamie Tait, either. He's
a dropout, too. He's about seventeen and he's been
hanging out with Copeland for the past year. He
lives on River Road. Fairly large family. Father in
prison for burglary. Jamie himself was once caught
shoplifting, when he was fourteen. And that's it."

"What number on River Road?" asked McGurk.

"I don't know," said Wanda. "I don't think Ed
knew, either."

"*I* know!" I said triumphantly. "I got it out of the
phone book last night."

And, just to prove it, I showed them the page I'd written my hunch on:

"Good work!" said McGurk. "So that's where we go next, men. Get your bikes."

Thirty minutes later, we were knocking on the door of 27 River Road. It was a shabby house with dirty windows and peeling paintwork in a neighborhood of huddled two-family houses and row houses. McGurk looked glum. Like most of the other houses, number 27 had neither garage nor shed, and very little land. There was no sign of Copeland's car parked anywhere near.

The woman who came to the door had the same slack, semismiling mouth as Jamie's. There was a cigarette drooping from it. The butt was very wet.

"Yeah?" she said, in a weary voice.

Two little kids had come out into the hall behind her. They peeked at us from behind her legs. They looked like Jamie, too, except they weren't smiling.

"Mrs. Tait?" said McGurk.

" 's me," she said.

"Is Jamie home?" asked McGurk.

"*Him!*" she said, with a snort that blew the ash off her cigarette. "*He* hasn't been home for a week. What d'you want him for?"

"We thought he might be able to help us find a missing cat," said McGurk, fixing her with a slitty stare.

If he'd expected her to betray any knowledge of Jamie's activities, he couldn't have been more wrong.

She just shrugged slightly and said, "He's staying with a friend of his. Len something or other. Way over on Pine Avenue."

McGurk thanked her politely and we left, feeling somehow deflated. I did, anyway.

But it takes a lot to deflate McGurk.

On the way back, we checked the Copeland house. The Thunderbird wasn't there, either. The garage door was wide open—the garage empty.

"They *must* have another hideout somewhere," McGurk said fiercely. "Another garage or shed or something."

He leaned on his bike, looking down, deep in thought, his freckles all clustering together.

"There's only one thing for it, men," he said, looking up again. "We cruise around on our bikes and see if we can spot that Thunderbird parked outside some other house. They probably have accomplices, anyway, if they're mixed up with the cat rustling."

"You think they are?" I said.

"Sure," he said. "I mean that's probably how they came to get their hands on Sheba and Natasha and the other cats they pretended to find."

"But—" Wanda began, looking puzzled.

"Before handing a bunch of cats over to the main rustlers," McGurk went on, "Tait and Copeland would cream off those that looked like they'd be more valuable to the owners than to the rustlers. I bet they didn't get more than five dollars a head from the rustlers. They were asking fifteen from the owners."

"But what about Ziggy?" I said. "The rustlers wouldn't want—"

"No, of course not!" said McGurk. "That was another bit of private enterprise. When Tait and Copeland saw how much they could make from the Pet Finders racket, they began to look around for other kinds of pets. Like the box turtle—"

"But how did they even *know* about Ziggy?" asked Wanda.

McGurk's eyes glowed with triumph then.

"Oh, that!" he said. "Easy. When they paid Ray Williams a visit last Friday, asking if he wanted to hire them to find Whiskers, they heard Ziggy chattering and screeching away. And Ray told them what the noise was. I checked this out with Ray on the phone last night. He even told them that it was a valuable bird."

"So when they saw Mrs. Berg in the supermarket yesterday—" Brains began.

"They jumped at the opportunity to swipe Ziggy," said McGurk. "Right!"

"Well this doesn't help us find him," said Wanda.

"No," said McGurk, getting on his bike, "so— like I said—we cruise around, keeping our eyes skinned for that old Thunderbird."

"And Ziggy," said Mari.

"And Whiskers," said Willie.

McGurk looked worried.

"I don't think we're gonna find either of *them*," he said. "Not unless we track down the Thunderbird first . . ."

Well, we cruised around for hours, but there was no sign of Copeland's beat-up car anywhere. By lunchtime we'd covered the whole of our side of town pretty thoroughly.

"We'll cover the other side after lunch, men," said McGurk, with a very determined gleam in his eyes.

And he's so thorough, we probably would have, too—until every street in town had been combed.

But there was no need for that, because, shortly after lunch, we were rewarded with the kind of breakthrough that all detectives hope for but very rarely get.

13 The Ransom Note

It was an afterthought, really. But it was an afterthought arising from McGurk's thoroughness.

"Before we start the second half of our patrol," he said, "let's check with Mrs. Berg. See if those jerks have been in touch with her yet about finding Ziggy. My guess is no. But we might as well check."

Mrs. Berg was sitting on the porch when we got there. The radio was on the table but it wasn't switched on. There was a folded sheet of paper under the radio.

She was strangely subdued. She didn't smile when she saw us, and she had this kind of hunted, frightened look.

McGurk didn't seem to notice this.

"Hi, Mrs. Berg!" he said, in a breezy, businesslike

tone. "Have you had a call from Pet Finders yet? About Ziggy."

Mrs. Berg shivered a little.

"No," she said, dully. "No, not yet . . ."

McGurk looked at us as if to say, "What did I tell you?" But Wanda was obviously more concerned about Mrs. Berg's health.

"Have you had any word from the police, Mrs. Berg?"

Wanda asked the question gently, quietly, but its effect on Mrs. Berg was alarming.

"Wh-what?" she said, staring up at Wanda and starting to twitch and tremble. "Oh, no! No! Not the police! They mustn't—oh, dear!"

Then she started sobbing.

We looked at each other.

Had she flipped?

She was quick to get control over herself.

"I—I'm sorry!" she said. "But—but it's been such a shock."

Then she pulled the slip of paper from under the radio.

"Here," she said, unfolding it. "I didn't find it until about half an hour ago. I'd left the car out in the driveway overnight. And someone—someone had slipped this behind the windshield wiper."

We stared at the paper. It looked kind of spooky, with all the different-sized words and letters that had been clipped out of newspapers or magazines and pasted there. It took me a second or two to realize that it formed a message. This message:

I HAVE youR biRD. It IS perFEcLLY
O.K. - so far. YOU will GET *it* BACK
if **you** *are* reasonIBLE & PAY me $500.
We *will* CALL 6:30 TONIGHT. If READY
to **Deal** just say YES then we'll LET
You know **next** STeP. If ansER is NO
- we *know* SOME **Pretty** hungry CATS
who'll ENJOY the bi**rd** for SUPPER and
THAT GOES for if you **Report** this *to*
the POLICE too.

McGurk's eyes were gleaming as he read the note.

Wanda sighed. "Well, at least it shows that Ziggy isn't flying around loose, Mrs. Berg. That he's still alive."

"Yes, but for how *long?*" wailed Mrs. Berg. "I— I can pay the money—if they give me time. But will they be patient?"

"Well," I said, "we know for sure now who's got him. Right, McGurk?"

I was thinking of one particular word in that note. He nodded.

"I thought you'd spot that, Officer Rockaway," he said. "And did you notice the switch from 'I' to 'we'?"

"Spot what, McGurk?" asked Willie.

McGurk ignored the question. He was too busy asking Mrs. Berg one of his own. In a very stern voice.

"You're surely not going to give in to this, ma'am," he said. "I mean you *must* let the police know."

Mrs. Berg gulped. "But you see what they say! If—if I call the police they'll kill Ziggy!"

"Not if we get to him first!" said McGurk.

"But *where*, McGurk?" asked Wanda. "I mean I have a good idea who it is. But we still don't know where they've hidden the bird. It could be here in town or it could be out in the country. We still don't have a clue—"

"*Don't* we? Huh! Hah! Wanda!" For a few moments it was like Brains was having some sort of fit. He'd turned very red in the face and was dancing from one foot to the other and waving one hand in the air, like he was in class at school and badly wanted to go to the bathroom. Even Mrs. Berg seemed to forget her own troubles as she stared at him.

"Officer Bellingham!" growled McGurk. "What's with you? Here we are, faced with a deadline and—"

"I know, I know!" said Brains, jigging faster than ever. "But, Wanda," he went on, turning back to her, "can you remember *now* where Ed told you the old Thunderbird was for sale?"

"Officer Bellingham!" McGurk growled again. "This is no time—"

"Think, Wanda, think!" Brains urged.

Wanda was frowning.

"Yes, well," she said, "I have a feeling he said somewhere over near Brackman Station—"

"Brackman *Swamp*?" yelled Brains, jumping—actually jumping—in the air.

"Why, yes," said Wanda. "I do believe—"

"*Jeb Lee!*" said Brains, turning to McGurk. "The guy we saw talking to Copeland and Tait. Jeb Lee, the junk dealer, with a place way off the beaten track, with a barn and—and—"

McGurk was grinning now. Broadly grinning and patting Brains on the left shoulder.

"Officer Bellingham," he said, "I do believe you've got it. It fits perfectly. Officer Master Brains Bellingham, I am now making you a knight—Sir Brains Bellingham."

"I kinda got to like being Master Brains Bellingham. . . ."

"Okay," said McGurk. "Sir Master Brains Bellingham, then. *Officer* Sir Master Brains Bellingham, you've done good!" He turned to Mrs. Berg. "You needn't worry anymore, ma'am. You'll get Ziggy back well before 6:30. So you can go ahead and phone the police as soon as you like. And when they come, tell them to check this note against the Pet Finders ad in the supermarket."

"Especially the spelling," I said.

Mrs. Berg was looking bewildered.

"But—aren't you going to stay?" she said. "And tell them yourself whatever it is you—"

"No, ma'am. Sorry!" McGurk said. "We've got to move fast! Men—grab your bikes and let's go!"

14 The Secret of the Barn

Brackman Station is on an old country road about two miles from the main Johnsonville highway. The branch railroad line that used to be there was torn up long ago, and the ticket office was converted to a regular house. There are a few more houses clustering around this one, and then the road goes on, twisting and turning and rising and falling through farmland until, about a mile beyond Brackman Station, it falls finally down along the side of Brackman Swamp.

Jeb Lee's place was on a spit of firm land at the side of the road, with the tall rushes of the swamp bordering it on the other three sides.

"Is *this* it?" McGurk asked Brains, as we rounded the last bend.

"Yes," said Brains, with a sigh of relief.

McGurk had been asking him the same question whenever he spotted a building of any kind near the side of the road, and I think Brains had started to worry about whether he'd remembered the route after all.

"It's certainly nice and secluded," said Wanda.

"*Nice*?" I said.

The place was anything *but* that. I mean it was not only an eyesore, but it was hard to focus, it was such a dump. Even now I find it hard to know where to start describing it.

Maybe it will be best to present a rough plan of it first. Like this:

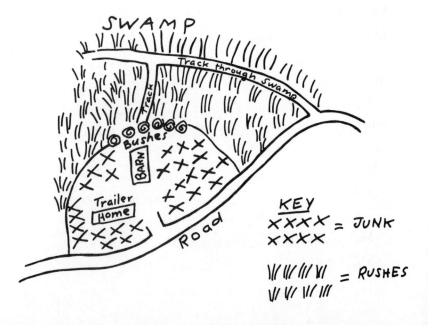

The junk was all over the place: old car engines; heaps of tires; rusted TV antennas; plastic bags, bulging and bursting, with more rusty metal showing through the holes; the outboard motor of a boat; the broken, grimy hull of a boat; a couple of crumpled yellow snowplows; the shells of four or five auto bodies; two or three cars with one or more wheels missing; two cars up front looking a tad less battered than the rest—but only a tad—with four wheels each and unshattered windshields, on which someone had daubed in white, 4 SALE."

There was no sign of Jeb Lee's pickup truck and no old Thunderbird.

"Looks like no one is home," said Willie.

Some of the windows of the trailer had been broken, and the holes stuffed with rags or pieces of plastic bags.

"We'll see, anyway," said McGurk. "Come on, men—but leave the talking to me."

Up until then we'd been standing on the road. Somehow even McGurk himself had seemed reluctant to go closer. We followed him, though, as he wheeled his bike up to the trailer and knocked on the door.

To everyone's relief, there was no answer.

McGurk knocked again, louder this time.

Still no answer.

"Good!" McGurk murmured. "That leaves us free to take a look around the barn."

The barn was the most solid structure in the place. It had lost most of its original dull red paint, but it looked in pretty good shape.

We left our bikes next to the two cars that were for sale.

"Ah!" said Willie, even before we'd reached the barn door. "Cats!"

When we did reach the barn door, even I could catch a whiff.

"It's locked," said McGurk, trying the handle. "Let's see if we can see anything through the windows."

We walked all the way around, but every first-floor window had been boarded up.

"Of course," said Wanda, "he *could* have a few cats of his own." She shuddered slightly. "Otherwise the place would be swarming with rats."

Willie sniffed and shook his head.

"No. No rats. No swarms of them, anyway." He sniffed again. "Cats, yes. Swarms of *them,* maybe."

McGurk turned to Mari.

"Officer Yoshimura," he said, "give us—"

She was already coming out with a long-drawn-out feline squawl.

McGurk waved her quiet and pressed his ear to the barn wall. He needn't have bothered. A faint but definite answering mewing came from inside, loud enough for us all to hear.

We looked at each other.

"They *could* be his cats," Wanda said again.

"There's only one way to find out," said McGurk. "The window up there is broken, but it doesn't seem to be boarded up. Officer Grieg?"

Wanda caught on at once. We were at the end of the barn overlooking the swamp. At one time somebody had trained a pear tree to grow against the wall, pinning its outspread branches there. It looked dead, but Wanda gave the trunk and two lowest limbs a tugging and said, "Seems firm enough."

And with that she began to clamber up the wall of the barn, using the branches as widely spaced steps.

"See anything, Officer Grieg?"

Wanda was right next to the window by now, peering in.

She suddenly gasped.

"Hey! There—there are stacks of *cages*! Small cages, like they use for chickens! Against the wall! And I can just make out—hey! They *are* cats!"

Something in her voice must have communicated

to the imprisoned creatures the fact that help was at hand. Without any encouragement from Mari, several of them began to wail.

"And—hey!"—Wanda called out again—"I think—on—on a table or bench or something—I think I can see a *bird cage!*"

"Is Ziggy in it?" asked McGurk.

"I—I'm not sure," said Wanda. "There's an old coat or sack or something, partly covering it."

"Officer Yoshimura!" said McGurk. "Aim it up there, through that window."

"Yes, Chief McGurk," Mari said. *"How* dare *you talk to me like that!"* she screeched.

Some of the cats raised their voices at that.

"Anything from the bird cage, Officer Grieg?"

Wanda shook her head. "No sound. But I think I saw a movement."

"Officer Yoshimura," McGurk began, "this time try a—"

But just then we heard the sound of a truck's engine around the front of the barn, followed by the slam of a door.

"Quick!" gasped McGurk. "Get down! He's here, I think!"

His words had been addressed to Wanda, but there wasn't time to see how she responded, because now there came the clump of footsteps and we'd all turned to see who was coming.

Suddenly, McGurk strode out to the corner to meet the newcomer, waving for us to follow him.

And it was a good move, too, because before Jeb Lee could reach the corner, the rest of us had emerged in a bunch, causing him to stop and giving Wanda the chance to get down in time.

Yes, it was Jeb Lee all right.

And there, on his own territory, between the rusting piles of junk, he seemed even bulkier and uglier than he had on Pine Avenue: like a great, bad-tempered bear, with little eyes peering out from a brutal, sweaty face.

"What goes on?" he growled. "Is them *your* bikes? Whaddya want, huh?"

15 The Collars

Earlier, McGurk had told us to leave the talking to him. But just at that moment, he seemed to have lost the power of speech. He was staring up at Jeb Lee with a half-open mouth, but no words were coming out of it.

So maybe it was as well that Brains disregarded the order. Looking up at the man pop-eyed, he blurted out his speech:

"Oh, hi, Mr. Lee! Hi! Remember me? I came with my father, Mr. Gerald Bellingham Senior, about a year ago, looking for a spare carburetor."

Jeb Lee stared at Brains, first with astonishment, then uneasily. Certainly without recognition.

"Huh—maybe you did—I don't recollect. Anyways, what do you want *now*?"

By this time, McGurk had found his tongue. With a quick, pleading glance at Brains that seemed to say, "Thanks, Officer Bellingham, but now will you please shut up?"—he smiled up at Jeb Lee and said:

"We're looking for some pedals, sir. For a bike. The rattrap kind?"

Jeb Lee suddenly seemed to breathe easier.

"You came to the wrong place," he said. "I only deal in auto parts. Now beat it. I'm a busy man."

"Yes, sir, of course," said McGurk. "Sorry to have troubled you. Have a nice day. . . . Come on, men!"

"Phew! That was a close shave!" said Wanda, as we pedaled our bikes back up the road.

"That was a good excuse you came out with, McGurk," I said. "He seemed to buy it, too."

"Yeah," said McGurk, with that old familiar gleam in his eyes. "But the time for talking's over. Now we know for sure where the cats and the parrot are, it's time to act."

He glanced back. Jeb Lee was nowhere in view.

"Act, McGurk?" said Willie. "How?"

McGurk said nothing until we'd rounded the bend, completely out of sight of the junk dealer's place.

"Right," he said, pulling up and dismounting. "Here's what we do. Officer Grieg and Officer Bellingham, go back toward town on your bikes as

fast as you can. Call the police as soon as you get
to a phone. Tell them what we've discovered and
where. Tell them where you're calling from and stay
there in case they need you for further information.
Go on! Right away! Every minute could count!"

"What about the rest of us?" said Willie, as Wanda
and Brains went on their way, pedaling furiously.

"We stash our bikes behind these bushes," said
McGurk, "and go back on foot. Keeping a low profile. Ready to act if it looks like Jeb Lee's about to
move the cats elsewhere. He might be more suspicious than he seemed."

So McGurk, Mari, Willie, and I cautiously made
our way back along the road. Following McGurk's
lead we bent double, ready to dive into the under-
growth at the side of the road. Luckily, there was
still no sign of Jeb Lee. When we reached the opening of the track through the swamp—shown on the
map—we were able to straighten up some and take
advantage of the tall rushes.

"How far are we going along here?" asked Willie.
The track was firm enough, but slightly soggy.

"Just to where we can get a good view of Jeb Lee's
place," said McGurk.

The best place seemed to be about fifty feet from
the road, at a point where a narrower path branched
off from the main one, leading toward the junkyard

itself. From this position we could see the whole of the back end wall of the barn and the side where the door was. Also the back of the trailer. The barn door still looked firmly shut, though there was no way of knowing if Jeb Lee had gone in there.

Willie was sniffing gingerly. "Pow!" he said, as he stood there, half crouched again, watching the barn door.

"What's wrong?" asked McGurk.

"This swamp," said Willie. "It sure smells!"

"What of?" asked McGurk.

"Garbage, mostly," said Willie.

"Yes," said Mari. "This man is a very dirty man. This is where he dumps his garbage. Look."

Sure enough, just beyond the edge of the narrow side track, nearer to the yard, patches and strips of white garbage bags showed through the rushes. And once our eyes were alerted to this, we saw glimpses of others, some white, some blue, some black. The sight of them seemed to help bring out the smell of rotting garbage.

"The guy's using the swamp as his own private landfill," I said. "I hope we don't have to wait here long. There's no telling what we might catch!"

"Hey!" said McGurk. "Look at this one!"

He had grabbed at some nearby rushes, parting them like a curtain and revealing a black plastic bag that had burst open. Something white was curling out, like a strip of apple peel.

Then, as I focused more clearly, I saw why McGurk was looking so excited.

"It looks like a flea collar!" I said.

The bag was several feet away from the firmness of the path, out of reach. There was an oily glint of water at the bottom of the rushes.

We looked at each other.

"Officer Yoshimura," McGurk said thoughtfully, "you're the lightest—" Then he changed his mind. "Hold it. I never send my officers where I wouldn't risk going myself. Officer Sandowsky, grab my belt at the back and hold tight while I lean over and reach out."

Well, I had to look away. One false move, one slip, and both McGurk and Willie would have gone flat on their faces in that foul-smelling swamp. But, after a short period of gasping and grunting, McGurk managed to get hold of the bag and draw it closer.

"There must be dozens of them!" McGurk murmured, as he plunged his hand in and drew out some of the flea collars.

They came in all colors. Most had names on them. Names like Kitty and Sugarpuss, Silvertoes and Sukie and Coco and Ralph—and Whiskers.

McGurk's face was radiant as he pulled this last
one out:

"Boy!" he gasped. "What a bunch of good hard
evidence! All ready for when the cops come and—"

"Listen!" I said. "Maybe this is them now."

There'd been the sound of a car engine, pulling
up, followed by the double thud of doors being shut.

Just then the barn door opened and Jeb Lee
walked out, closing it behind him.

"It's Copeland and Tait," said McGurk, as the two
youths came up to Lee at the side of the barn.

They kept their voices down at first, too low for
the words to be distinguished, but sounding angry.

Then Jeb Lee raised his high enough.

"You'll get paid!—Anytime now—Don't worry—
Hey, and I *could* charge ya rent, you know!—What
for? For that dumb bird is what for!"

"Okay!" said Copeland. "Keep your shirt on!
We—he's here now."

There'd been the sound of another engine. Then
we saw a medium-sized van slide into view, between
the barn and the trailer.

McGurk put the bag of collars down.

"Come on, men," he whispered. "Let's try to get closer."

Crouching again, he led the way along the narrow path to where the ground sloped up to the yard. There were some stunted bushes there. We crouched down behind them, only a few yards away from where Jeb Lee was standing with the two youths. All three had their backs to us as they watched the van driver get out. He was a tall man with dark glasses and a leather jacket.

"How many ya got this week?" he asked.

"Twenty-three," said the junk dealer.

"That all?"

"Yeah, well," said Lee, "these jerks have been goofing off, lately. Anyways, twenty-three ain't all that bad. That'll be three hundred fifty dollars."

"Okay, okay!" snapped the newcomer. "Twenty-three fifteens. That's three hundred forty-five, pal. Not three hundred fifty."

He began peeling off bills from a huge roll. The other three couldn't take their eyes off it. There was a brief, greedy silence. Then the newcomer looked up and, without handing over the money he'd counted out, he said:

"Well, don't just stand there! Open up and lemme check the merchandise!"

It was just as Jeb Lee was turning to the barn door that Willie let out an ear-splitting "Ouch!"

He was clutching the back of his neck. We found out later he'd been bitten by a deer fly.

All four men turned.

"What was that?" one of them said.

"Seemed to come from those bushes," said another.

Valiantly, Mari threw a duplicate "Ouch!" in the direction of the trailer—but it was too late. Jeb Lee and Copeland were already scowling down at our four scared faces.

Then McGurk showed his quality as a leader.

"All right!" he said, straightening up and clambering up the bank. "We're making a citizen's arrest. Stealing and transportation of cats. Larceny of valuable bird. And attempted extortion."

If he'd burst in on them with an automatic rifle and a SWAT team, it couldn't have had a more startling effect.

Lee, Copeland, and Tait just gaped.

The van driver hurriedly stuffed back the wad of bills and glared at the others.

"Jerks!" he said. "Letting a bunch of kids get wise to you! Wait till the boss hears about this, Lee!"

He walked toward his van. I guess he thought that the only thing that *could* be done now was to kill the four of us and toss our bodies into the swamp—and he didn't want any part of that.

Lee himself seemed to realize the hopelessness of his position. But he made one last attempt to settle the matter.

"Hey, Art!" he called out. "Wait! We'll *buy* them off! We'll give the kids these jerks' share." The driver shook his head and started the engine. "*My* cut, too!" Lee yelled. "They can have the whole three hundred forty-five—Right, kids? How about it?"

McGurk's expression was stony.

"Attempted bribery and corruption of arresting officers," he said. "In front of witnesses. You might as well—"

He broke off at the sound of another car pulling up. (And blocking off the van's exit, as we soon found out.)

"All right, you!" barked the voice of Patrolman Cassidy. "Cut the engine and get out! And no funny business. There's two back-up cars arriving momentarily."

McGurk swayed slightly. I thought he was going to faint. He'd known all along that the police would be on their way, of course. Even so, it had taken some guts to do what he'd done.

Anyway, he pulled himself together and called

out, "Hi, Mr. Cassidy! The other three are round here, in back of the barn."

Well, the other three *were* around there. But even as McGurk spoke, Tait and Copeland went plunging down the bank and into the swamp, where they floundered around helplessly in their panic.

"They won't get far," said McGurk.

Patrolman Cassidy was now approaching, his hand on the butt of his gun, his eyes on Jeb Lee and the van driver. Wanda and Brains were peering around the corner of the barn, where they'd been told to stay.

Jeb Lee made one more desperate attempt to wriggle out of the matter.

"What's with you, officer?" he said. "We ain't done nothing wrong!"

"Oh, no?" said Mr. Cassidy. "Open up that barn and we'll see about that."

"There's nothing in there," said Lee.

"There's a bunch of stolen cats in there," said the patrolman. "According to reliable information received. Plus a two-thousand-dollar stolen parrot."

"Baloney!" said Lee. "What would I want with a bunch of cats? And a *parrot!*—Hear that, Art? The guy's nuts! And anyways, where's your search warrant, *officer?*"

That seemed to stop Mr. Cassidy for the moment.

"I can soon get one," he said.

"Get one then!" Lee jeered.

"And give you the chance to get rid of the evidence?" said Mr. Cassidy.

"No warrant, no open up," said Jeb Lee, folding his arms.

"I gotta get out of here!"

I *still* don't know whether it was Ziggy himself or Mari. She flatly refuses to say.

But the effect on the bystanders was instant.

"If that wasn't a parrot, I'm a girl scout!" said Mr. Cassidy. "Coming from in there, too. And *that,* Jeb Lee, gives me Probable Cause to search the barn without a warrant. Do you want to open up and make it easier on yourself, or do I shoot off the lock?"

Jeb Lee suddenly sagged. Either Mr. Cassidy's words or the sound of more cars arriving decided the matter for him.

"Okay, then," he said. "But I didn't know nothing about the parrot being stolen. Just taking care of it for a couple of—uh—*friends,*" he added, nearly gagging on that last word.

As McGurk said later: "I sure wouldn't like to be in those two jerks' shoes if they get put in the same cell with *him!*"

16 McGurk Looks to the Future

So that was another victory for the McGurk Organization—a double one in a way—and of course McGurk was very pleased.

"In fact you could even say it was a *triple* triumph," he said, later that week, when we heard that the cat rustling ring in New York had been busted—thanks to the information coughed up by the man named Art. "I mean they were collecting stolen cats from the whole of the tri-state area."

"Yes," said Brains. "Mr. Cassidy was telling my dad that hundreds and hundreds of cats were involved."

"And thousands and thousands of dollars," said Willie wistfully.

I knew how he felt. The police tracked down the

owners of all those twenty-three cats, thanks mainly to the sackful of flea collars we told them about. And just about every one of those owners wanted to give us a few dollars' reward. Especially Ray Williams, who was over the moon at getting Whiskers back— a thinner and hungrier and dirtier Whiskers, but otherwise none the worse for his ordeal.

"Come on, McGurk," said Ray. "At least take the fifteen dollars I'd scraped together for those two jerks."

But McGurk wouldn't hear of it.

"Buy Whiskers a new collar with it," he said. "A couple of cans of his favorite food. A catnip mouse."

"But why won't you take it?" asked Ray.

"Yeah!" said Willie.

"Because what I said at first still holds good," said McGurk. "We don't take penny-ante cases. And if we took this from you, that's what it would go down as."

"But—"

"It's no use arguing, Ray," said McGurk. "I mean we're the guys who turned down three hundred forty-five dollars to look the other way."

Well, his logic was all haywire, but there's no way anyone can get McGurk to change his mind when it's all made up. He even refused a reward from Mrs. Berg.

She came to see us in McGurk's basement the morning after the showdown. We'd just been thrashing out the wording to add to our notice: the extra piece describing the latest success.

Should it be, "Catnappers Confounded" or "Parrot Purloiners Apprehended"?

McGurk liked them both, but not enough.

"We need something that covers the *whole* case," he said.

Finally, we hit on something that did just that. But even then, when I thought it was all settled and I'd typed it out neatly, McGurk had to make an amendment in his curliest corkscrew handwriting.

> *Crooked*
> COMPETITORS
> CREAMED

Mrs. Berg stopped by while I was taping this to the bottom of our notice.

"And a very good job you made of it, too!" she said. "I've come to thank you all."

"How is Ziggy now?" Wanda asked.

"Delighted to be back home," said Mrs. Berg. "He's just started to speak up again."

"Did he learn any new words from the thieves?" asked Mari.

"No, thank goodness!" said Mrs. Berg. "But I came here with a small reward. I can't afford—"

"Close your purse and forget it, Mrs. Berg," said McGurk, suddenly lighting up. "I've just thought of what would be the best reward of all!"

"What's that?"

"That you let us visit him for half an hour a day—"

"Oh, but you'd be welcome to do that anyway!" said Mrs. Berg.

"—so that I could teach him to read people their rights," McGurk continued. "Like if anyone attempts to steal him again, he'll be able to scare the daylights out of them."

Well, it's been more than a week now, and he's still working on it. So far, he's been able to get Ziggy to say, in a voice uncannily like McGurk's, "You have the right to remain silent—"

And you never know. Mrs. Berg says Ziggy is likely to live another forty or fifty years. So the chances are that in all that time someone *will* try to swipe him.

"So that even when we're old and gray, the McGurk Organization will *still* be fighting crime," McGurk said. "Indirectly, anyway."

"Oh, why stop there, McGurk?" said Wanda sarcastically. "With new developments in veterinary science, Ziggy might live to be well over a hundred. We could be helping to prevent a crime long after we're all dead and gone!"

"Gosh, yes!" said McGurk, sitting back and slowly rocking in his chair, his hands clasped behind his head. "Good thinking, Officer Grieg! *Very* good thinking!"

I guess it made him feel kind of immortal. . . .